The Shimmering Ghost of Riversend

Norma Lehr

Lerner Publications Company • Minneapolis

The map on page 6 is by Aldo Abelleira.

This edition of this book is available in two bindings:
Library binding by Lerner Publications Company
Soft cover by First Avenue Editions
241 First Avenue North
Minneapolis, Minnesota 55401

Library of Congress Cataloging-in-Publication Data

Lehr, Norma.
    The shimmering ghost of Riversend / Norma Lehr.
        p.   cm.
    Summary: Eleven-year-old Kathy, spending the summer with her aunt
in her old family mansion, is visited by the ghost of a beautiful
woman who died in the nineteenth century.
    ISBN 0-8225-0732-3 (lib. bdg.)
    ISBN 0-8225-9589-3 (pbk.)
    [1. Ghosts—Fiction.] I. Title.
PZ7.L53273Sh   1991
[Fic]—dc20   90-19941
                                                                  CIP
                                                                   AC

Manufactured in the United States of America

1 2 3 4 5 6 7 8 9 10 00 99 98 97 96 95 94 93 92 91

To Jason and our little comet, Austin

CHAPTER
1

"Why can't Snuggles come with me?" Kathy pleaded, clutching her fluffy white dog around the middle. "We've never been away from each other for more than one night in six years." She stared up at her mother through the open car window. "That's almost half my life. Don't you think Snuggles is going to be lonely without me? She would have fun in the country. I'll take good care of her."

Mrs. Wicklow shrugged. "I know you would. That's not the problem. We've been over this before, Kathy. Aunt Sharon's got a cat. And Snuggles chases cats. It's not fair to your aunt."

"But the cat doesn't have to see her. I'll just keep her in my room. No one will know." She pulled

Snuggles close to her face and squooshed her possessively. "I will have my own room, won't I?"

"Yes, Katherine Ann. You know you will."

When her mom called her Katherine Ann and her nostrils flared in that certain way, Kathy knew *that was that.*

Mrs. Wicklow's face softened as she reached in and took Snuggles from Kathy's arms. "I hope we packed everything you need for at least a month," she said, using a finger to count the luggage on the back seat. "Did you get your drawing pad and pencils?"

Kathy nodded without looking up. "I brought them, but I won't need them. I won't be drawing."

"You might change your mind, Kitten," said Mr. Wicklow, turning the key in the ignition. "Wait until you see the foothills. Wicklow Manor is in Riversend, one of the most historic and beautiful towns in the famous California gold country. Or should I say infamous?"

So what, Kathy thought. No matter what her dad said, she wasn't going to draw pictures of a strange place she already hated. Why should she try to please her parents when they were sending her away from home, her friends—and even Snuggles —because her mother had decided to go back to work?

If she wasn't an only child and maybe had a sister

for a pal, things might be different. Then she could stay home instead of tramping through the woods with some weird aunt she barely knew. (She'd heard her mother refer to Aunt Sharon as weird.)

Kathy reached out and rubbed Snuggles on the head. Mrs. Wicklow waited until Kathy finished, then pulled her close and kissed her. "I'll miss you, honey," she said, her voice breaking. "Be sure and call when you get settled. And be careful."

Careful? What did her mother mean by that?

"Cheer up, you two," her dad said, patting Kathy's knee. "It isn't the end of the world." He glanced at his wife. "She won't be living on a mountain peak, Diane. She'll be staying with my sister in a Victorian house that has been in our family for over a hundred years. It should be a terrific experience for her."

As the car pulled away from the curb, Mrs. Wicklow waved. "Drive carefully, Dan."

Kathy waved back at her mother and Snuggles until she couldn't see them anymore. When they reached the turnoff to Highway 80, her dad turned east.

"I'm glad this is happening," he said, nodding. "It's time you and your aunt finally got acquainted. She's my only sister and she's never had children of her own." He glanced over at Kathy. "She's really looking forward to this."

"How do you know?" Kathy said, trying to swallow the lump in her throat.

9

"Because she's the one who suggested that you two spend some time together. She was living on the East Coast and she hasn't seen you since you were a baby." He studied her face with a look of approval. "You resemble her, you know. Same dark hair and green eyes."

Kathy pulled a strand of hair in front of her face and went cross-eyed trying to see the color, then quickly brushed it back behind her ear. So that's where I get the brown hair, she thought. Great! I look like the weird relative living in Riversend.

She slumped down in her seat. The car zoomed by tall buildings and subdivisions. The scenery slowly changed to empty lots, then large meadows filled with yellow and purple wildflowers. Kathy stared out the window and thought about home.

Maybe her mom's new job wasn't the only reason her parents were sending her away for the summer. Maybe they didn't trust her to stay home by herself—because of those dreams. The message dreams. She sometimes saw things in her dreams that later happened, like when her mother lost a ring and Kathy dreamed that it was wedged between two boards on the deck.

Kathy began to whistle, softly at first, then a little louder. Miss Collins, her teacher, was a good whistler. Kathy wanted to be good too.

"Just practice every day," Miss Collins had said

on the last day of school, "and before long you will have it mastered."

The country would be a good place to practice, Kathy nodded to herself. When she got to Riversend, she'd look for some quiet spot of her own where she wouldn't have to worry about anyone hearing her. Or about strange dreams.

Maybe the summer wouldn't be wasted after all.

CHAPTER
2

"It's not far now," her dad said excitedly, scanning the hills and meadows. "I love this country. We came here when we were kids, Sharon and me."

When they reached a clump of eucalyptus trees drooping in the midday sun, he stopped the car. "Here's the entrance to the old place."

Kathy felt a grabbing in her stomach. The towering trees formed a tunnel over the gravel road and she forgot all about whistling. She wanted to beg her dad to turn around and head back, but instead she said, "I think the trees are ugly."

Her father took his foot off the brake and the car climbed slowly up the hill, passing an old graveyard on the way.

"Look," he said, pointing.

Kathy stared at the old tombstones, gray and leaning, then slid down in her seat and crossed her arms tightly across her yellow T-shirt. "Is this graveyard part of the manor?" she asked uneasily.

"Sort of. Your ancestors are buried there. Later, when you feel more at home here, you might want to walk down and read some of the markers. Find out who these people were. In the old days people were buried close to where they had lived."

She would never go into that creepy place with the broken metal fence and the tall weeds. And she would never feel at home here. Besides, why should she care where those dead people were buried? She didn't know them.

The car bumped along for a few minutes, then her dad shouted, "There she is—the old manor."

Kathy sat up and looked out. Then she gasped. The big brick and wood house was spectacular. Wrapped with long white balconies and verandas and dozens of windows all trimmed in red, it stood on a hill burned amber by the summer sun. From the roof a gable shot up with a fringe of carved wood hanging from its eaves like old lace. At the far left was a red brick tower capped with a witch-hat roof, and below two windows glared silver.

Kathy reached around and grabbed her drawing

pad from the back seat and riffled through the pages. "Look, Dad," she exclaimed. "I drew this."

Her dad took the pad and studied the picture, comparing it to the manor on the hill. "This is really a fine drawing, Kathy. Did you do it from a photo?"

"No—no," she said excitedly. "I just drew it."

Her dad turned to her and lifted an eyebrow. "You've never seen a photo of this house?"

Kathy shook her head hard.

"Come to think of it," he said, "I don't believe we have one at home. But I'm sure your grandma does. Did you see one at her house?"

Kathy shook her head again, but this time slowly. She studied her fingers as they twisted the hem of her shorts. "I've never seen a photo anywhere." She added softly, "I just drew it out of my head."

"Then I must have given you a vivid description of the old place," he said.

She didn't bother to tell her dad that he hadn't. Every time she asked him what the manor looked like, he'd say, "Just wait until you see it. I could never do it justice by trying to describe it."

Then how had she been able to draw it? Even the brick tower was in the right place. She glanced up at the house, then took her picture back. Should she try to make her dad understand that she'd drawn this from her imagination?

14

Better not. Her dreams had caused enough trouble.

Kathy slipped the drawing back into the tablet as the front door of the manor flew open and a tall woman with dark hair stepped out. She hesitated as she stood under a freshly painted sign that read WICKLOW INN. "Hello, you two," she called, shading her eyes. "I've been watching for you."

Kathy's father slid from his seat and stood up. He came around to Kathy's side of the car just as his sister reached them. The two hugged each other, and for a moment, Kathy felt a twinge of jealousy.

"Kathy," her dad said, taking her arm and drawing her into the circle. "This is your aunt Sharon."

Her aunt reached over to give her a hug, then hesitated. "You probably don't remember me, Kathy. It's been a long time since we've seen each other. I have a hug for you, too, but if you'd rather wait, I understand." She reached in her skirt pocket and pulled out a small printed card and handed it to her. Kathy took it and read, GOOD FOR ONE HUG.

At least she wasn't pushy, Kathy thought. She didn't like being hugged by strangers. And that's exactly what her aunt was — a family stranger. She looked up and Sharon was smiling. Kathy felt like smiling too, but instead she bit on her lower lip.

"I'm so pleased you're here," Sharon said, holding out her hand. "Do you suppose we can shake?"

15

Kathy wasn't sure, but when her dad gently nudged her arm, she grasped Sharon's hand. It was warm and soft.

"I really will appreciate your company, Kathy," Sharon said. "It gets lonely up here sometimes." She turned toward her brother. "Especially at night."

Her dad looked surprised. "You mean there's still . . ."

Sharon shook her head and frowned. "No, no—at least I don't think so," she said quickly.

What was that all about? Kathy wondered, feeling that twinge again. They must have secrets. All brothers and sisters shared them. Her friends back at home did. Sometimes she whispered her secrets to Snuggles and other times they went into her drawings.

She reached into the back of the car and pulled out the bag that held her art supplies and quickly stuffed her tablet in. If she was lucky, her dad would forget about her drawing. The thought of him telling Sharon about the picture made Kathy want to turn and run. Her dad joined Kathy and removed the rest of the bags from the car.

Well, this was it. No turning back now. She could say *No, I don't want to*, but that wouldn't work. She'd tried that. The plans for her summer vacation had been made. She didn't like it, but what could she do? She grabbed her bag.

The adults went on ahead, chatting together while Kathy lagged behind and struggled up the slope. When she reached the steps of the manor, she dropped down on the first step. The instant the back of her legs touched the weathered wood, she felt strange—crowded, like somebody was sitting next to her and pushing. A cold breeze brushed the side of her face and she jumped up. "What was that?" she blurted out.

"What was what?" Sharon asked, looking concerned.

Kathy rubbed her cheek with her knuckles. "Something cold hit my face."

Dan Wicklow raised his brows. "What did it feel like?"

"An icy wind," Kathy said irritably. "How could it be cold when it's so hot today?"

"It was probably just some flying insect," he said, moving over to the steps and examining the spot on her cheek where Kathy pointed. "There's no mark there. I guess you'll live." He smiled reassuringly. "Let's go inside and get something cold to drink."

"There's some iced tea and lemonade," Sharon said brightly. "And I baked granola cookies especially for your arrival. How does that sound?"

Cookies and lemonade did sound good. Kathy nodded and picked up her bag.

She waited until her dad and aunt went in, then

17

she glanced around, searching for flying bugs. When she didn't see any, she stepped down and looked up at the front of the manor again. In her picture she'd colored the trim around the windows red—almost the same shade of red as the trim above her.

Was the picture a message like her dreams? She hadn't wanted to come here in the first place. If that drawing was some kind of message, she sure didn't want to stay in Riversend to find out what it meant.

She climbed the steps warily. At the door she turned and looked back to the spot where she had felt the cold breeze. She shuddered, then stepped inside, letting the door close behind her. Taking a deep breath, she started down the dark hall.

CHAPTER
3

Kathy's dad and aunt disappeared through the far door to the left beyond the staircase. As she hurried along after them down the dimly lit corridor, something soft brushed against the calf of her leg. She reached down and a tiny sandpaper tongue licked her fingertips. The cat!

"That's Gypsy," her aunt said, poking her head out the door. "You can bring her into the kitchen, if you like."

Kathy didn't "like." It was the cat's fault that Snuggles had to stay home. "Go away," she said, brushing the cat aside.

The cat backed off and crouched against the wall.

"That's right. Just keep your distance," said Kathy, trying to look stern.

She stepped back, then peered up the carpeted staircase. The stairs were steep and narrow, with a spindle banister made of dark, polished wood. Even though the red carpet on the steps looked clean and bright, a musty odor there made Kathy wrinkle her nose.

"Gross," she moaned. "The guests won't like that." Kathy sniffed with distaste, turned abruptly, then marched down the hall. Well, that was Aunt Sharon's concern.

In contrast to the dark hall, the kitchen was sunlit and cheery. Her dad and aunt sat across from each other drinking tea at a heavy wooden table. "You still have that same cat!" her dad exclaimed.

Kathy turned quickly. The cat had followed her in.

Her dad reached over and gave Gypsy's head a rub.

"Isn't she beautiful?" Sharon said affectionately. "She's been such a good friend to me all these years."

How old was that cat? It sounded like Aunt Sharon had had her forever. In the light, Kathy had to admit that Gypsy's coat was pretty. Her fur was orange and white with—oh no!—a white star between her eyes.

It couldn't be. Kathy started to go for her drawing tablet again, then stopped. She'd done a charcoal drawing of a cat last week. And she had drawn it with a star between its eyes.

"She likes you," Sharon said. Gypsy wove in and out between Kathy's ankles.

Kathy didn't move or say a word. She just stood there like a statue until the cat padded over to the braided rug in front of the sink and curled up. But Gypsy didn't close her eyes. She kept staring at Kathy.

"Don't be surprised if you find her on your bed some morning," Sharon continued. "She has a knack for finding her way into the rooms of people she likes."

"How about when the guests arrive?" Kathy's dad asked. "What will you do about her then?"

"I'll just have to warn them," said Sharon. She laughed quietly. "Gypsy's wise, though. Unlike other cats, she doesn't bother those who don't want her. She has a way of knowing such things. Sometimes I think she's psychic—especially around the Wicklow place." Dan Wicklow and his sister exchanged knowing looks again, but this time Kathy ignored them. Let them have their little secrets. She was thinking about the picture she had drawn. Was the charcoal cat another message?

Aunt Sharon passed the plate of cookies to Kathy, then poured a tall glass of lemonade over ice cubes. "Made it fresh this morning," she said. "If you like it, I have a crate of lemons in the cellar and I'll show you how I make it. Then you can drink it whenever you want." She turned to her brother. "I use maple syrup as a sweetener. Perhaps Diane wouldn't agree," she sniffed. "But believe me, it's much easier on the system than sugar."

"Still into nutrition, huh?" her dad said with approval. "Your dining room should go over big. The foods you ate in the sixties are fashionable now."

A health food nut! That's what Kathy had heard her mother say about her aunt. ("No—a health enthusiast," her father had corrected.)

"I'm still a health enthusiast," Sharon said now to Kathy's dad. "Menus won't be a big problem here. The problem is hiring the right help in the kitchen."

"You'll help your aunt, won't you, Kathy?" her dad said. "Didn't I hear you tell your mother you wanted to learn to cook?"

Kathy had said that. But here in her aunt's strange kitchen, she froze. What kind of cooking did her aunt do? What if Sharon asked her to make something so healthy she couldn't eat it?

Her dad and aunt were both staring at her, waiting for her reply. She glanced from one to the other, nibbling on her lip as she tried to think of a polite thing to say. She did want to learn to cook—but from Aunt Sharon?

"Kathy," her dad insisted. "Am I right?"

"Right," Kathy said, forcing a smile. "I can help you, Aunt Sharon, until you find someone." She plunked down on the rug next to Gypsy and picked the raisins out of her granola cookie.

As her dad and aunt turned back to their discussion about Wicklow Inn, Kathy took the time to study her aunt. She was really pretty. Kathy couldn't understand why her dad thought she looked like Sharon. They had the same dark hair and green eyes, but her aunt didn't have any dumb freckles across her nose.

When her dad spoke, Kathy turned her attention to him. He looked like Sharon. It was easy to tell they were brother and sister. Kathy knew Sharon was older, but she sure didn't look it. If Kathy was lucky enough to be as pretty as her aunt when she grew up, that would be just fine—she'd settle for that.

"Come on, Kitten." Her dad picked up her bags. "Let's get you settled in a room of your own before I leave. There are seven bedrooms here. Which one does she get, Sharon?"

"There are six guest rooms," she corrected him. "Follow me."

Kathy and her dad trudged up the stairs behind Sharon, following her as she turned on the landing and then went on to the room directly over the kitchen.

"I've given her the Rose Room, Dan. There's such a lovely view from the balcony."

A balcony! Without bothering to look around

the room, Kathy dropped her bag on the four-poster bed and opened the glass doors leading outside. A wooden balcony stretched from one end of the house to the other. White wicker chairs sat on the balcony at each of the other four entrances. Aunt Sharon was right. What a view!

Kathy could see across the whole valley to the hills on the other side. It looked like a postcard with the two church spires and all the houses and low buildings in the distance. She took a deep breath of the summer air and closed her eyes. When she opened them, they focused closer to the house. Pine trees stood like sentries on each side, while closer to the balcony, the branches of a huge oak tree rested on the railing. Below, a river at the bottom of a steep slope behind the manor flowed vigorously over white rocks and boulders.

"This is the shady side," her aunt said, joining her near the railing. "This oak tree will protect you from the heat. I hope you'll be comfortable here."

Kathy was so impressed with the beauty around her that a spark of creativity surged through her, nudging her into a daydream. She was lost to the moment, when her dad's voice suddenly interrupted.

"I'll be taking off now," he said.

Kathy twirled around to face him.

"But you—we just got here," she said.

"I know. But it's a long drive home. When your

mother and I come to pick you up, we'll stay overnight. How does that sound?"

It sounded like forever. "When?" she asked, choking back tears.

"It won't be as long as you think. I'll bet you won't want to leave when it's time. I know I never did." He looked around the room wistfully, then turned to Sharon. "When I come back it'll be just like old times, huh?"

He kissed Kathy on the forehead and made her promise to call home at least once a week, assuring her that he and her mother would do the same. "How about coming down and seeing me off?" he asked, hesitating at the door.

Kathy looked down. Gypsy was near her feet. The cat had followed her up to the room and out to the balcony. Kathy shooed her away.

If Kathy went downstairs now, she didn't think she would be able to stop herself from jumping into the car.

"That's okay," she said, not looking up. "I just want to stay here on the balcony." She turned and gazed unseeingly over the valley.

Her father's footsteps faded down the stairs. When the front screen door slammed, Kathy jumped. A moment later the car door shut. She was fighting to swallow the lump that had formed in her throat when suddenly her eyes focused on a boy dressed

25

in cutoff jeans and an old straw hat striding across the slope directly below her. He was carrying some sort of a flat pan that flashed in the sun, and he was shouting to someone near the river. Kathy was so busy trying to figure out what the boy was doing that she didn't hear her aunt come back out.

"That's Todd Malone," Sharon said, moving next to her. "He lives down by the river with his grandfather. We can walk down there later and I'll introduce you to him, if you like."

Kathy felt the color rush to her face. She hoped her aunt didn't think she was interested in boys. She'd never met one yet she really liked. But she was filled with curiosity about where he was going — and about what he was going to use that pan for. She stared down at the tumbling river.

"Okay," she said to her aunt, surprising herself. "I'll change into my tennies and we can go now."

CHAPTER
4

When they were just a couple of steps out the front door, Sharon stopped and pointed to a high grassy mound a short distance to the right. "That's the root cellar."

Kathy's eyes followed her aunt's finger. "Where?" she asked. "I don't see a cellar."

"This way," her aunt motioned. They tramped through the grass to the mound, where a weathered plank door lay at an angle against the dirt. "This is where I keep the fruit and vegetables so they won't spoil." She reached down and gripped the metal handle. Bending her knees, she pulled up and the old door opened with a creak. "It stays cool down there in the earth."

Kathy edged over near the opening. The same musty odor that had been on the staircase in the hall suddenly hit her nose, making her eyes water. "What's that smell?" she asked, shaking her head. "I hate it."

"I know what you mean," said Sharon. "You have to get used to it." She looked thoughtful for a moment. "I remember the first time I smelled it. I was about your age." She studied Kathy. "It was strong for me then, almost overpowering. Guess you don't want to go down and look around, huh?"

"No way," Kathy said. But she did inch her way over, trying to see into the dark hole. "How do you get down there?" She pinched her nose, squatted down, and peered in. "Oh, I see—brick steps. Do they go to the bottom?"

Sharon nodded. "When I came here in the spring, the original wooden steps were rotten, so I laid the bricks. They're solid and safe if you decide to try them."

"How big is it down there, anyway?"

"From the floor to the top, it's about six feet high," said Sharon. "And if you're measuring across, it's about four feet each way."

Kathy stood up as her aunt moved to close the door. "Is that where you keep the lemons?" She glanced up at the glaring sun and brushed her hair back from her face. A glass of her aunt's lemonade sounded good right now.

"Yes. But we still have some in the kitchen." Sharon stepped aside. "Would you like to try to close the door?"

Kathy grasped the handle. Sharon let go and Kathy let the door down slowly.

"Good job," Sharon said. "It takes a lot of strength to close it carefully like that. Most people just let it drop with a thud."

Kathy knew she was strong. Exercising on the metal bars in the schoolyard had built smooth muscles in her arms. She felt her right arm with the palm of her left hand. "I am strong for my size," she said proudly, gripping the handle again. "Can I try opening it now?"

"Give it a try," said Sharon.

Kathy bent over and tugged with both hands, but the door wouldn't budge.

"It helps if you bend your knees. It's a matter of balance." Sharon spaced her feet. "Use the big muscles in the back of your legs. That way you won't hurt your back."

Following her aunt's directions, Kathy was surprised to find that the door opened without much effort. She smiled triumphantly. "That was easy." She did a little dance in a circle and Sharon laughed.

Kathy closed the door again, then brushed her hands off. "Okay," she said, standing up straight. "Let's go down to the river."

29

When they were a few feet away from the mound, a shiver passed through Kathy. She turned and looked back, but she didn't stop. A couple of feet later, it happened again. This time she didn't even bother to turn, because the sparkling river below held her attention. As they neared the bottom of the hill, a harsh grating sound filled the air.

"Whoa—what was that?" she asked, holding her hands over her ears.

"It's Mike's jackass." A voice came from behind her.

Kathy spun around and stared into the dark eyes of a boy a half-head taller than her. He wore a tattered straw hat that shaded his face and neck.

"No, it's not," a shaky voice protested.

Kathy turned in the other direction, this time to face an old man crouched near the river. He was swirling water around in a slope-sided pan that looked something like a pie plate. He wore a faded felt hat, its brim pinned up in front with a huge safety pin. A red bandanna was tied loosely around his neck, and his dusty Levi's were tucked into high boots.

He set the pan down and frowned at the boy. "Nugget is my burro and he doesn't like it when you call him names."

"Jackass is not calling him names," the boy said, brushing past Kathy and her aunt. "It's in the dictionary as another name for a donkey."

"Gosh darn it. He's no donkey either," the old man persisted. He squinted up at the boy, who was standing next to him with his back against the sun. "Old Nugget was a burro when I got him and that's what he'll always be." He turned back to swishing the water in the pan.

Sharon walked on down. "Is the river giving up any of its gold today, Mike?"

Gold! So that's what the pans were for. But in rivers? Kathy had only heard of getting gold from gold mines.

"Some," the man replied as he struggled to get up. "Well now, if it isn't Miss Sharon." He twisted the end of his handlebar moustache as his bright blue eyes focused on Kathy, and she could see by his sunken lips that he didn't have any teeth. "And I'll betcha a leather pouch full of gold dust that this young one here is the niece you've been telling me and Todd about."

He brushed the dirt from the knees of his pants and removed his hat. His white hair clung damp to his forehead, then fell to his shoulders like thin yarn. "Pleased to meet you, Miss Wicklow." He made a wide flourish with his arm as he bowed from the waist. "And this here is my grandson, Todd. Well, he's really my great-grandson. His daddy was my grandson."

Todd gave a forced smile to Kathy and her aunt, then folded his arms tightly across his blue tank top.

31

Mike's burro, somewhere off to the right, made another frantic call, starting Todd and his grandfather arguing again. Kathy watched intently as their conversation heated up. The old man's rubber face, tanned and creased, twisted in frustration as he tried to make his point.

Todd listened to what his grandpa had to say, then hunched his shoulders and turned away. "Okay, he's a burro." He pushed his straw hat back, letting loose strands of blond hair. As he started to walk away, Kathy heard him mumble, "Burro is Spanish for donkey and a donkey's a jackass."

"Where is Nugget?" Kathy blurted. "Can I see him?"

Todd glanced back over his shoulder. "If you want. Follow me—but hurry up." He headed toward a cabin a short way down the river.

"Go on," Sharon said when Kathy looked over at her for permission. "It's all right. That's where they live. I'll talk to Mike for a while, then I'll head on home. Take your time. I'll be in the kitchen when you get back."

Kathy hesitated. Did she really want to go with this kid? This mouthy know-it-all guy? But she'd never seen a burro, except on TV—or a donkey—or a jackass. She looked over at Mike then ahead at Todd. "Wait a minute," she called after him. "Don't walk so fast."

Todd shrugged. "That's what I hate about girls,"

he grumbled as she came up alongside him. "They can never make up their minds. That's why they're so slow. 'If you stew about making up your mind,'" he sing-songed, "'you lose valuable time.'"

"Yeah," Kathy said, out of breath. "Who says?"

"My grandpa, that's who—Upstream Mike."

"Your *great*-grandpa," Kathy corrected him. "You heard what he said back there."

"It doesn't matter what kind of grandpa he is," Todd said, stopping and glaring. "He's mine. I just call him Mike, anyway." He began walking again, this time scuffing his sneakers in the loose dirt. "But to newcomers like you," he added, "he's Upstream Mike."

"I suppose he can tell me himself what he wants to be called," Kathy said. "He's your grandpa, but it's his name."

Todd faced her. "Well then, go ahead and ask him."

"Okay, I will."

Neither of them spoke until Kathy spotted a lean-to behind the cabin. Two long gray ears edged with black poked out. "Is that Nugget?" she asked, running over to the fence that corralled the burro. She reached in between the slats and petted his head. Nugget lifted his lips over his huge teeth. "Look. He's smiling. Todd, look."

"Yeah, he always smiles when someone pets him. Crazy, isn't it?"

"I think he's adorable," Kathy said, climbing up

and pressing her head against his fuzzy brow. "But why does he make such an awful noise?"

Todd filled a bucket from the river and poured the water into a trough inside the stall. "He brays because he wants attention."

"He must get lonely here all by himself," she said softly, knowing just how he felt. "Why do you keep him penned up? Why can't he be free?"

Todd clanked the bucket down. "Because he goes into town on his own if we don't pen him. Then I have to go after him. Mike takes him into town on weekends to let the tourists give their kids a ride and take pictures. I guess Nugget likes all the petting, because that's where he heads every time." He took a ladle from a cistern of water and slurped a drink. "How come you ask so many questions, anyway?"

Kathy reddened. "Because how else can a person find out information?"

"By reading," Todd said, wiping off his chin with the hem of his shirt.

"What book would tell me about Mike letting kids ride Nugget?" Kathy jumped down from the fence and started back.

"Okay," Todd said quickly. "That wouldn't be in a book. But it might be someday when I write it."

Kathy turned, shoving her hands into her pockets. "You're going to be a writer?"

"I already am." Todd looked confident. "I write down the stories Mike tells me."

"What kind of stories?" Kathy had never known a writer before.

Todd narrowed his eyes. "Scary ones. About ghosts and spirits and stuff."

"Yeah. How old are you anyway?"

Todd opened his mouth in surprise. "What's that have to do with anything?"

"Nothing," Kathy said with a shake of her head. "I was just wondering." She glanced over at the river. "Are you trying to get gold out of there too?"

"I've got lots of gold," he said, standing up straight. "And I'm twelve." He gave Kathy a measured look. "How old are you—ten?"

Kathy's eyes blazed and her chin jutted out. "I'm eleven and a half." She stomped off.

"Wait a second," Todd commanded.

Kathy half turned her head but kept on going.

"I said I wrote scary stories—about ghosts."

Kathy shrugged. "So?"

"I said Mike told me about them."

"I heard you." She kept on moving, but Todd caught up with her.

"Some of the stories are about the old Wicklow place."

Kathy stopped dead in her tracks. She turned and faced him with her hands planted firmly on

35

her hips. "Are you saying that there are ghosts up there?"

Todd blinked and looked away. "I didn't say that."

Kathy began to run, stirring up clouds of dirt behind her.

"Come back down to the river tomorrow," Todd called after her. "Mike will answer your questions. He'll tell you everything you want to know."

CHAPTER
5

Back at the manor, Kathy stormed through the kitchen door and dropped into a chair across from Sharon, who was busy snapping green beans into a pot. "I hate him," Kathy said. She jumped up and grabbed a glass from the counter. "Is there any more lemonade?"

Sharon motioned to the refrigerator. "What's wrong? Did Todd give you a bad time down there?"

Kathy poured a glassful, then gulped it down. "I could just strangle him. A person tries to be friendly, and all he does is tell lies and act rude."

"Sounds like you got the tail end of his anger," Sharon said. "He was piling it on Mike when we got there, so he must have turned it on you. But I wouldn't take it personally. He's having a difficult time at home right now. That's why he's here with his grandpa."

"You mean he has a *real* home with parents and everything?" Kathy raised one eyebrow. "That's hard to believe."

"His mother lives in Placerville, about a twenty-minute ride from here. His father died a couple of years ago and his mother just remarried. I hear Todd's having a hard time adjusting. His stepfather has two daughters who stay with him, and Todd's not used to living with girls."

"That's awful," Kathy said sympathetically. "It must be terrible to lose your dad. But he doesn't have to take it out on me."

"You're right," her aunt agreed. "Most of the time he's a nice guy. I've always thought that Todd has the qualities of a good friend if someone wanted to pursue it. Could be that he's a little suspicious of you because you're about the same age as one of his new sisters. When he gets to know you better, I'm sure he'll trust you."

Kathy set her glass down in the sink. "Well, I don't trust him. He lies." She faced her aunt. "He said there's ghosts up here. That isn't true, is it?"

With her back to Kathy, Sharon placed the pan of green beans on the stove. "What did he say exactly?"

"Just that—and if I wanted to know more, Mike would tell me."

Sharon was quiet for a moment and Kathy began to feel uneasy. "Well? Is it true? Does Wicklow Manor have ghosts?"

"I heard a few stories when I was your age. I'm not sure if I believe them. Todd's dad and Mike were living at the cabin then, and Mike told me some spooky tales." She turned around. "Mike's ancestors lived at Riversend when the first Wicklows were here. A lot of what Mike says is hearsay—stories handed down from his relatives."

The sun was fading in the kitchen window, casting strange shadows across the tile floor. "Well, I'm going back down to the river tomorrow and ask Mike," Kathy said, rinsing out her glass. She whistled softly as she reached for a towel.

Sharon puckered up and tried to join her, but only air passed through her lips, and she and Kathy burst out laughing.

"I used to be able to whistle," Sharon shrugged. "But I guess I lost it." She wiped her hands on her apron. "Come on. I'll give you a tour of the old place before dinner."

They passed through an adjoining door into a wood-paneled dining room with a high, beamed ceiling. At the far end was a massive fireplace made out of rough white stones like the ones in the river.

Around the room, six unevenly spaced tables were covered with linen tablecloths.

"This town gets thousands of visitors each year," Sharon said. "I'm counting on lots of those visitors staying here." She adjusted one of the tablecloths.

Kathy noticed that the chairs were old, probably just right for this house, but it was strange that none of them matched.

"I know they don't match," Sharon said. "But I wanted to keep it all as authentic as possible. I picked them up at local attic sales for a good price." She motioned for Kathy to follow her as she headed for the hall. "I didn't have much money left over after I had all the plumbing redone."

She held the parlor door open and Kathy walked in. The walls were covered in gold brocade and the wood floor was so shiny it reflected the light that filtered through the lace curtains. Kathy stared at the crystal chandelier hanging from the ceiling. She rushed over and sat on a high-backed velvet chair and rested her feet on the matching stool.

"It's all so beautiful," she said, jumping back up and crossing to a heavy rolltop desk. "Whose is this?" She ran her fingers over the smooth wood.

"That belonged to the master of this manor—the man who built it, James Wicklow, our respected ancestor."

"Then who's that?" Kathy exclaimed, stepping

back and staring up at the portrait of a woman. The woman wore a pale blue dress, and her red hair was pinned with flowers.

"That's Jenny Wicklow—James Wicklow's daughter. One of the mistresses of the manor."

"Look at her ring." Kathy pointed at Jenny's pale finger. "It looks like a gold wreath."

"Lovely, wasn't she?" Sharon said. "She died when she was quite young. She's buried in the old family plot down the road. You passed the graveyard on your way here this morning."

Kathy remembered the creepy place full of weeds, but right now she was intrigued by the oil painting hanging above her. Something wistful in Jenny's eyes saddened her. "She doesn't look very happy."

"She had a tragic ending," Sharon said. "She drowned in the river."

Kathy's eyes widened. "This river? Mike's river?"

Sharon nodded slowly. "No one knows what really happened. She must have fallen in and was swept away by the current."

"That's awful," Kathy gasped. "She probably couldn't swim."

"In the spring and early summer, that river can be treacherous," Sharon said. "When the snow melts in the mountains, the water comes rushing down. Chances are Jenny would have drowned whether she knew how to swim or not."

She crossed to the window and gazed out. "Back when Jenny lived here, life was hard. It wasn't long after the gold rush of 1849, and the town hadn't settled down yet. There were strangers around here and strange happenings going on."

Sharon held back the curtain. "Not far from here is Sutter's mill, where James Marshall picked up that first bit of gold in 1848 and history was made." Dropping the curtain, she went to the desk and sat down. "James Wicklow made a fortune in Riversend. He was a banker. He's written up in some of the history books over in the Placerville library."

Kathy was impressed. "You mean he was famous?"

"Not famous like John Sutter or Mr. Marshall, but he was a prominent citizen and a very powerful man around these parts." She stood up. "Shall we get on with the tour?"

Kathy trailed after her aunt through two more beautifully decorated rooms before they headed upstairs. The four guest rooms on the second floor were filled with window seats and skylights and satin comforters on high brass beds. Each window was covered with light lace curtains. Kathy knew that she had never seen such a magnificent place before.

Sharon guided her down the hallway. "Did you peek at your bathroom yet? I put in all the modern conveniences. When the guests start to arrive, you'll probably have to share my room. But for now, enjoy."

"Wait," Kathy said, pointing toward the end of the hall to the small square landing inside the arched entrance to the tower. "Those winding stairs. Where do they go?"

Sharon kept on walking. "We're not going up there."

"Why? It looks neat."

"I know, but the steps are broken."

"Can I see?"

"Not now, Kathy," Sharon said, ushering her into the Rose Room. "I want you to see this bath."

A claw-foot tub sat in the middle of the room on the large pink marble floor. Kathy let out a squeak. "It's great! I can fill it with bubbles and soak."

"I thought you might like it," Sharon said proudly.

Kathy walked out and draped herself across the four-poster bed. "I feel just like a princess."

"You look like one, too," Sharon said warmly. "You have all the Wicklow airs about you." She hesitated a moment, then turned to leave. "I'll go down and finish fixing dinner. If you want to unpack, dinner should be ready by the time you're through."

"When those steps in the tower get fixed, can I go up?"

Sharon frowned. "Those circular stairs lead up to the tower suite. I'm not planning to have them

43

repaired—not now, anyway. So please stay away," she said with a warning tone. "They're dangerous. There's a huge gap where the steps are missing. All that's left in that section now is an old wooden handrail. I've hired a carpenter to come by next week," she added thoughtfully. "He's going to board up the entrance to the tower before the first guests arrive."

"But if he fixed the steps, then you'd have another room to rent," said Kathy.

"Perhaps someday that will be possible, but not now."

Boarding the entrance didn't make sense to Kathy, especially since it led to a tower room. Her aunt must have her reasons, though. Maybe she didn't have enough money to fix the stairs. Too bad.

"Have you ever been up there?" Kathy asked as her aunt was leaving.

"Yes. I was there a month or so ago." She turned abruptly and it was clear she didn't want to pursue the matter. At the door she stopped. "Just promise me you won't try to go up there." Without waiting for Kathy's reply, she left.

Dinner was tasty, considering most of it was vegetables from the garden. Sharon had spiced them with herbs and baked them in a casserole covered with melted cheese. Kathy dug in with an

44

appetite triggered by the clear country air. When she finished, she used thick slices of homemade bread to mop up the juice from her plate. "I was really hungry," she said apologetically.

"Eat all you want," said Sharon. "But save room for dessert." She returned from the fridge with a bowl of fresh strawberries. After spooning them over angel food cake, she topped it all off with whipped cream.

Kathy was in heaven, but it wasn't long before she placed her fork down next to her plate and leaned back. Covering her mouth with her fingers, she yawned. It wasn't quite dark yet, but the lengthening shadows made her eyelids heavy.

Sharon smiled at Kathy. "I'll take care of the dishes. Go on up to your room and relax. Tomorrow is going to be a busy day. I've hired Todd to come up and put in the gravel walkways. Maybe you could help him."

The tiredness suddenly left Kathy's eyes. "Isn't there anything else I can do?"

"That's the big project for tomorrow," Sharon said, clearing the table. "If the two of you work together, it will go faster." She studied Kathy's face. "Of course, if you really don't want to . . ."

Kathy knew she should help when her aunt asked. But work with Todd? She thought about how bossy he was, then remembered about his father dying and his mother remarrying. Suddenly she softened. "I will, I guess," she said, feeling tired again. "But if he tries bossing me around . . ."

"This is your place, Kathy. Remember that. Tomorrow Todd will be on your turf and I'm sure he'll behave himself."

Kathy stretched and nodded. "Right. He'll be on Wicklow property. And if he doesn't shape up, he'll have to go home." With a comforting sense of power, she climbed the stairs to her room. After filling the bathtub with water and bubbles, she soaked, thinking about home. She wondered how her mom and dad were and if they missed her.

Using a thick towel to dry herself, she walked out into the room and slipped on her nightgown. Gypsy was lying on the comforter. Kathy picked her up and set her out in the hall. "You're not welcome in here," she said irritably, missing Snuggles. "If my dog can't be in my room, I don't want you in here." She closed the door in Gypsy's face.

She crossed to the French doors and stood on the balcony. The night was warm. Too warm to sleep inside. Would her aunt permit her to sleep outside? She went downstairs to find out.

Later, as she spread a sleeping bag on the weathered planks, her body was tired, but her mind was a-tingle. She lay down and stared up at the bright stars winking at her from the black sky. A bird croaked in the nearby oak while a yellow moon rose over the mountain. Before long Kathy was lulled to sleep by the steady sound of crickets singing.

She awoke with a start. Gypsy, with stiff legs and a hunched back, was pressed against the railing of the balcony making a weird moaning sound. Kathy peered over at her. "What's wrong?" she asked sleepily.

The moon had climbed high in the sky. As Kathy gazed past Gypsy, a gray mist rose up the side of the hill. A woman in a billowing hooded cloak, carrying a swinging lantern, scurried to the top, stopped a moment to glance back, then rushed on.

The night was absolutely still, but as the woman approached the house, the silence was broken by the sound of her rapid breathing. Kathy, wide-awake now, sat up and rubbed her eyes. She peered down, but she couldn't see the woman's face beneath the hood. When the woman had almost reached the back door of the manor, she stared up at Kathy with terror in her eyes, spun around and ran over to the mound above the root cellar, then disappeared. The low, heavy mist receded down the hill, and as it did, Gypsy relaxed.

Kathy waited and watched, but the woman didn't return. "Who was that?" she asked the cat. A scurrying sound alerted Gypsy again. Kathy pulled the sleeping bag over her face. She peeked out just in time to spot a squirrel jumping from the balcony railing to a tree limb. Kathy reached out and pulled Gypsy next to her. Squirming back into a comfortable position, she gave a sigh of relief and fell into a deep sleep.

CHAPTER
6

The sun was up when Kathy was startled awake by the grinding sound of a dump truck emptying gravel. Gypsy was gone, so Kathy rolled up her bag and went inside. As she dressed, she thought about the cloaked woman she'd seen during the night. She hurried downstairs to tell her aunt.

But the kitchen was empty. The table was set with cereal, bread, and fruit. Propped against the bowl was a note.

> Didn't want to wake you but I had errands to run. Be back soon. Please pay the man for the gravel. The check is in the top drawer of the rolltop desk.
> Love Sharon

A knock on the back door sent Kathy racing to

the parlor. She found the check, then hesitated a moment while she stared at Jenny Wicklow's portrait. The sadness in Jenny's eyes brought the strange event of the previous night into focus. A loud, insistent rap at the kitchen door jarred Kathy back to the present, and she hurried to answer.

When Kathy opened the door, it wasn't the delivery man waiting to be paid, it was Todd Malone. His arms were crossed over his chest and his straw hat was pulled down over his eyes.

"Is your aunt here?" he asked suspiciously, trying to see past her.

"Hello, Todd," Kathy said, determined to be nice. "My aunt Sharon's gone for a while, but the gravel's here, so we can get started." She opened the screen door and stepped out.

"What do you mean *we* can get started?"

She waved the check under his nose. "I'll be back as soon as I pay the delivery man." She marched off in the direction of the truck with an air of authority. When she returned, Todd was already placing large river rocks as a border for the gravel.

"How many walks are we going to make?"

"I thought you were going to tell me. You're one of the mistresses of the manor now — Mike said."

Kathy placed her hands on her hips. "He's right," she said. "But I didn't plan this project. You'll have to tell me what to do until I catch on."

"Just follow across from me with those big ones," he said, motioning to the wheelbarrow filled with rocks. "I'll tell you when to stop."

They worked together silently for a while, but Kathy had to share last night's experience with someone. Todd must know who the woman was and what she was doing out on the hill in the middle of the night. She eyed him. She didn't feel like sharing if he was going to be rude.

Suddenly, she felt as if someone was watching at her elbow. A cold shiver ran through her. She looked over her shoulder, but no one was there. "I saw a woman last night," she blurted out.

"Yeah—so?" Todd moved ahead on his knees. "What's that got to do with anything?"

"Well, it was strange. She was running up from the river and she had on a black cloak—and she had a lantern, and it was the middle of the night."

Todd stopped and squinted up at her. Then he grinned. "Too bad. It won't work."

"What won't work?"

"Your story."

Kathy looked confused. "It's true. I was out on the balcony," she insisted. "And this woman came running up looking scared."

"Sure, sure." Todd made a face and shook his head. "And you're trying to scare me, but it won't work."

51

"I'm not trying to scare anyone," Kathy said, puzzled. "I thought maybe you knew who she was."

"I do," said Todd matter-of-factly. "And so does your aunt—and Mike—and I guess now you've heard the story too. You just figured I haven't. Sorry." He went back to setting stones.

Kathy jumped up. "I don't know what you're talking about."

"Your stupid story about the Wicklow ghost."

Kathy opened her mouth to speak, then closed it. She looked at him sideways. "That was a ghost?"

Todd stood and faced her. "Isn't that what you're trying to tell me?" He pushed his hat back and Kathy could see his laughing eyes.

"You're a big fat pain, you know," she said. "I don't want to talk to you anymore. Let's just work."

"That's okay with me," he said, kneeling back down.

They worked silently. After a while Todd looked up. "Mike wants me to ask you to come for dinner tonight. Maybe you can tell him about your ghost."

Kathy was pleasantly surprised. "Dinner? What time?"

"You better ask your aunt first," Todd suggested. "It'll be dark when you come home." He grinned demonically and widened his eyes. "You might meet up with some strange woman wandering around on the hill."

"You're not funny," she said, but he might be right. "I'll ask."

"No problem. She'll let you come. Your aunt likes Mike." He smiled innocently. "And she thinks I'm a nice kid. Don't worry—someone will walk you home."

Sharon called later to say she wouldn't be back until evening. "Will you be all right?" she asked.

"Sure," Kathy said. "I can take care of myself."

"I'm over in Placerville," Sharon explained, with an edge to her voice. "There's a problem with one of the permits needed to open the inn." She hesitated, and Kathy could hear the rustle of papers. "Seems I filled out the wrong forms and now I'm waiting to talk to someone who can help me."

"We got two of the walks finished," Kathy said proudly. "But we didn't get gravel in the one that leads to the root cellar. We had to quit. It got too hot."

"That's great," Sharon said, trying to sound cheerful. "How did you and Todd get along?"

"Okay, I guess. Todd says Mike invited me for dinner. Can I go?"

Sharon heaved a sigh. "That would be wonderful. Then I won't have to hurry. But be sure someone walks you home. When the sun goes down, it's almost impossible to see the chuckholes when you climb back up the hill."

Kathy wanted to tell her about the woman in the cape, but Sharon sounded like she was in a hurry. "I'll be careful," Kathy promised. "See you later."

She hung up, then headed for her room, whistling as she went along. At the foot of the stairs, she stopped short. That awful smell made her cough and move back. The last thing she wanted to do was put her foot on the bottom step. Reaching for the shiny banister, she stretched her leg up past the first two steps.

A deep sigh echoed behind her. She turned quickly, but no one was there. Racing up the remainder of the stairs, she rested on the landing before she turned around again. When she looked down, a mist like the one that had covered the hill the night before rose up from the floor and formed a gray ball on the bottom step. Kathy blinked in disbelief as the ball shimmered, then separated into dark particles that quickly disappeared.

She squealed as something pushed against her leg. It was Gypsy. Reaching down, she picked up the cat. "Did you see that? I don't know what's going on around here," Kathy said out loud. "But I think I better find out."

CHAPTER
7

As Kathy neared the cabin, she could see Mike stooped over a smoldering fire. He was stirring something in a black pot hanging on a tripod. "Hello, Mr. Upstream," she greeted him. "Thanks for inviting me to dinner." She peered into the pot. "Are you fixing a barbecue?"

Mike straightened, stopped stirring, and tapped the ladle against the rim of the pot. The drippings from the spoon caused the fire to spit and hiss and send a finger of smoke spiraling up past his head.

"You can call me Mike," the old man said, wiping his hands on a faded bib apron. "Everyone around here does—and this is no barbecue." He winked at Kathy. "This here is campfire vittles." Bending over, he took a huge whiff of the steaming broth. "Ahh," he sighed. "Mulligan stew. My specialty." His eyes sparkled when he looked at Kathy, and she felt right at home.

"I could smell it all the way over here," she said, licking her lips. "It makes my mouth water."

"Well, it won't be long now," he promised. "Your taste buds are in for a real treat."

The cabin door swung open and Todd came out with a dish towel bunched up in his hand. "It's the outside cooking that makes it good. Mike's stew beats any barbecue I've ever had." He gave the picnic table a swipe with the towel. "Everybody's on their own down here," he said, eyeing Kathy. "You'll have to go in the cabin for your bowl and spoon."

Todd went in and she followed. The cabin was cluttered with old jars and bottles of odd shapes and colors. Against the far wall, a row of blackened pans hung on rusty nails. Kathy ran her fingers over a bright, woven blanket that covered the single chair beneath a high window.

She spotted a clear, tube-shaped bottle filled with water and flakes on the windowsill. "Is this gold?" she asked.

"Yep," Todd replied. "You can hold it if you want." He handed it to her. Kathy hesitated.

"Take it," he said. "It won't break. And what if it does? There's plenty more where that came from."

Kathy took the bottle and held it tightly. Todd pushed her arm up to the window. "When you shake it and hold it to the light, you can see all of the flakes."

Kathy's eyes widened. The flakes floated around in the water like the snow in a paperweight she had on her desk at home. "I'd die for this," she said. "Do you suppose Mike would show me how to get gold from the river?"

Todd dropped his hand from her arm and shrugged. "Ask him. He'll be panning all day tomorrow." He headed for the door. "Let's go. I'm hungry."

She searched through two cupboards before she saw a bowl, then she found a spoon in the drawer under the sink.

When she got outside, Nugget cried harshly. Kathy grinned. "He must know I'm here." She plunked her bowl and spoon down on the weathered table, then hurried around back to give him a hug.

"Seems you like that old critter," Mike said warmly when Kathy returned.

She nodded. He smiled and Kathy could see he was wearing his dentures.

"That burro just loves attention," he said, making a whistling noise through his teeth. "The next time we go into town, you're sure welcome to tag along." The whistle came again and he shook his head. "Gosh darn it," he said, frowning over at Todd.

"I'm taking these things out. Why you make me wear them when company's coming I'll never know. If a person can't talk right or eat right then what good are they?"

He went inside, then came back and stood in the doorway holding a pint jar filled with gold-flaked water. He smiled as he dropped his teeth in. "Here's where they belong, by golly." He chuckled. "Where I can keep an eye on them. Soaking them in here makes them the most valuable choppers in the county."

Kathy and Todd had just enough time to exchange grins before Mike hollered, "Soup's on." He filled their bowls with chunks of meat and potatoes. With a corner of his apron, he lifted hot biscuits from a pan and placed one on top of each bowl of stew. "Now dig in," he ordered as he joined them at the table.

Kathy downed two bowls, then gave up.

"Come on," Mike insisted. "You just got started."

"Whoa," she groaned, patting her middle. "I'm full."

"Me too," Todd agreed. He stretched his arms and sighed.

Mike shook his head. "Then you'll have to wait on me." He gummed a potato, then picked up his bowl and slurped the remaining soup through his stringy moustache. When he was through, he sat back.

"Now you two can clean up." He pointed toward the fire. "The water's hot and ready."

Kathy and Todd washed and dried the dishes, took them back to the cabin, and hurried over to join Mike by the fire. They sat down and crossed their legs. Mike was busy whittling the end of a thin branch into a point with his pocketknife. He shoved a marshmallow onto the pointed stick and handed it to Kathy. His eyes, reflecting red from the coals, gave him an eerie expression.

"Well, Missy," he said, studying her. "I hear tell you've seen the ghost."

Mike's bluntness caught Kathy off guard and she stared at him curiously, wondering what she should say.

Todd nudged her. "Go on. Tell him," he said. "He'll believe your creepy story."

Kathy flashed him a dirty look, then hurriedly explained to Mike about the woman on the hill with the lantern. She rushed on to tell him about the ball of shimmering mist she'd just seen on the bottom step of the staircase. "I know Todd thinks I'm making it all up," she said, glaring at him. "But I swear it's true."

The smoke from the fire suddenly blew in her face, making her eyes smart. Todd jumped up to get another marshmallow.

"Well, you don't have to cry about it," he said.

59

"I'm not crying."

"Leave the girl alone," Mike said sharply. "Or you might be asked to leave. This new mistress of the manor and me have some serious talking to do."

Todd sat down and Mike waited until they were all settled. "Now," he said, looking into Kathy's eyes. "Let's get down to bedrock.

"Seems like as long as I can recall and from what I've been told, it's the young ladies of the manor that gets the visitations. Personally, I've always figured that the ghost wandering that hill is a banshee, but it's not everyone in town who agrees with me." He paused a moment to make sure he had their full attention.

"A banshee?" Kathy asked. "What's that?"

Mike's eyes peered out of a face as creased as an old hide. "They're a kind of ghost," he said. "But not the kind you ever want to meet up with. Seems they attach themselves to their families and come around when there's going to be a death."

"A death?" Kathy shuddered. "Who's?"

"Depends," the old man said, reaching into his shirt pocket and removing a pipe. He tapped it sharply on a rock, then sucked on it thoughtfully. "Mostly it's some member of the family. But it's also been known to come back to gather up a close friend of the family." He narrowed his eyes and stared over at Todd, who popped a burnt marshmallow into his mouth and nonchalantly licked the sticky mess from his fingers.

Mike took a deep breath of the night air. "It all started a long time ago, when the first mistresses of Wicklow Manor lived up on the hill. They were your great-great-great-aunts," he said, figuring it on his gnarled fingers. "And two beauties they were. Miss Jenny with her flaming red hair, a healthy, witty girl, and Miss Lora, the dark-haired one, a brisk, strong-minded woman.

"When those two sisters went into town, they got the attention of every man around these parts. It was said that men deserted their work to come crowding around them, for a more beautiful sight was not to be seen." He stared up toward the manor wistfully, then shook his head.

"The trouble began not long after their daddy died. Their mama was already dead, and their brother, Daniel—your great-great-great—well, one of your grandpas anyway, had left for the city to build up his fortune. It was 1860. Some of the madness of the gold rush had passed, and this country was turning into orchards and vineyards. Young Daniel wasn't much interested in farming, so he turned the responsibilities of the manor over to his older sisters and left by the first stagecoach headed west."

"Daniel's my dad's name," Kathy said brightly, smiling at Mike. "He must have been named after our ancestor."

"Of course he was," Mike said quickly. "Daniel is a good Irish name. It's one to be proud of—though I don't know that I agree with what young Daniel did, leaving all that work behind for his sisters. But the two women worked hard to keep the land up and folks saw less and less of them.

"Then, one day in the dead of winter, a drifter came by the manor looking for work. He was a rough-looking fella, but word has it that he was as handsome as Clark Gable. I suppose when the sisters opened the door that cold morning both of them most likely swooned at the sight of him since they—"

"Clark who?" Todd interrupted.

Mike stirred the coals with his stick. "Don't you youngsters ever get to the movies? He was Rhett Butler in *Gone With the Wind*."

Todd glanced over at Kathy and they both shrugged. Mike gazed into the fire and was silent.

"Go on, Mike," Kathy said to him eagerly. "Please."

Mike nodded. "Well, those sisters were kindly as well as beautiful. They hired that passerby to help around the place, but proper ladies that they were, they insisted he get a room in town and come to the manor when he was needed.

"They say the fella obliged, but he must have been a blackguard at heart, because he immediately courted after both Lora and Jenny, and both sisters set their sights on him." Mike looked perplexed. "Can you beat that? There wasn't a man around these parts who wouldn't have given up his claim just to dance with one of those lovelies, my grandpa included, and this no-account stranger comes along and . . .

"Well, it wasn't long before townsfolk passing the Wicklow place could hear the sisters arguing. And it wasn't much after that, probably early spring, when the two ladies didn't go into town together anymore. If there were errands to attend to, it was Lora who shopkeepers remembered seeing. Whenever they asked about Jenny, Lora would just nod politely and mumble that everything at the manor was fine. Then she'd rush off.

"Lora was the oldest and everyone said she was leaving Jenny at home with the drifter, then sneaking back to spy on them." Mike paused and chuckled. Then he grew serious.

"If both the mistresses loved that fella so much that they wanted to marry him, I figure they must have revealed to him how big their dowries were. They were left a right good sum when their daddy died."

"What's a dowry?" Kathy asked.

"A dowry," Mike explained, "was the money a

woman brought to her husband in marriage. That was the tradition in those days."

"Then I'll bet their dowries were big," Kathy said. "My aunt said that James Wicklow was a rich banker."

"That's right," Mike agreed. "It was rumored that those sisters each owned nuggets weighing over thirty pounds, and that's not counting the gold dust they kept in their leather pouches."

Todd shoved another marshmallow on his stick. "When are you going to get to the good part about the murder?"

Mike shot him a leveling glance. "Just hold your horses, boy. Tales like this one take some telling."

Todd sighed. "Then should I get more wood? Pretty soon we won't be able to see."

"You don't need to see to listen," Mike said. "All you need to do is be quiet."

Mike lit his pipe and glanced at Kathy. She was still listening attentively. "Things got stormier and stormier up on the hill. The sisters were arguing constantly and when they attended church, folks noticed they were careful not to touch as they sat in their pew.

"Eventually, everything came to a head. One dark night in April, so they say, Jenny, who had finally won out, raced down the hill to meet her suitor on the riverbank, and Lora followed her. Another argument took place, a worse one this time, and in a fit of frenzy Lora pushed Jenny into the rushing waters. Then she ran off with the stranger.

"Some folks said that Lora had planned to kill Jenny all along. That way she could offer both of their inheritances to the drifter. And there was never an ounce of dust or a single nugget of gold found at the manor after that."

A chilly wind passed by Kathy and she shivered. "That's awful," she said. "But if it really happened that way, why haven't I ever heard about it?"

Mike sighed deeply. "I suppose, Missy, a murder in the family, even that far back, is not something family members are quick to talk about."

Kathy wasn't convinced. "Someone must have seen Lora again?"

"Nope. Not hide nor hair," Mike said firmly. "That's what makes it all so strange. She murdered her only sister, left the home she cherished, and ran off with a scoundrel." He pursed his lips and snorted. "A mighty shame, I'd say. She must have been crazy."

Kathy didn't know what to think. The whole story was such a tragedy. "Where did they find Jenny?"

"Lodged between two boulders down where this river turns and runs into the south fork of the American River—a spot we call Riversend. Two miners found her there and brought her into town.

She was thrown across the back of one of their horses like a sack of grain."

Kathy felt a little sick. "She's buried down at the graveyard," she stated sadly, repeating what Sharon had said. "I wonder where Lora's buried."

"No one knows," Mike said, "and they probably never will."

Todd jumped up. "I think it's all a bunch of goofy stories. Nobody knows for sure what happened to Jenny—or Lora."

Mike got up and stamped on a coal that threatened to ignite a twig. "If Lora didn't murder her sister, then why is she back here wandering the hills as a banshee?"

Kathy moved closer to the fire. First the dreams, then the drawings, and now the ghost—or the banshee. Kathy was ready to cry. What was she going to do? She didn't want to be one of the mistresses to get a visitation. She looked up to see Todd motioning for her. "Come on," he said. "Let's go."

The coals were turning gray. Kathy looked out into the inky darkness. "Don't worry," he said. "I've got a flashlight."

Kathy ignored him and turned to Mike. "Do you think the woman I saw was Lora?"

"Come on," Todd repeated, tugging on her arm. "I've got to get up early tomorrow."

66

She shook her arm free. "Mike," she persisted, and her blood seemed to race to her heart. "If Lora's back, why do you think she's here?"

"I believe there's good ghosts and bad ones," Mike said somberly. "I think you've got one of the bad ones up there on the hill. That house unleashed some terrible force, and I don't believe a Wicklow that stays there is safe in their bed." He gave the fire a rough poke and stood up straight. "The mistress who's got to be warned now is Miss Sharon. I've got a strong feeling that banshee's come back to get her."

CHAPTER
8

"You don't believe all that stuff, do you?" Todd said on their way up to the manor. "It's just a bunch of hundred-year-old gossip."

Kathy ran along breathlessly, trying to keep up with him. "What about the banshee?"

"It's an old wives' tale. Every time Mike tells it he adds something new."

Kathy stopped to catch her breath. "What was new this time? And slow down. What's your hurry?"

The beam from Todd's flashlight cut through the darkness, then focused on Kathy. He stopped and waited for her to catch up. "The new part is about your aunt Sharon," he said. "And I don't think you should warn her, no matter what Mike says."

"But what if she's in some kind of danger? What if we both are? What if that woman with the lantern is really the ghost of Lora come back as a banshee?"

"She's not Lora," Todd said, shaking his head. "Mike's a storyteller. He's been doing it for years. Folks around here come to the cabin just to hear him spin these yarns. So do the tourists. He's what they call 'local color.'"

Kathy shrugged. "I think I should tell her about last night, though."

"Sure. Go ahead," Todd said. "Tell her about the woman, not a ghost. She was probably somebody from town out searching for her lost dog or cat."

"With a lantern and wearing a long cape on a hot night? I doubt that."

Todd jumped a chuckhole and held the light down so Kathy could see. "If she's got to be warned, then let Mike do it. They're his stories, not yours."

Kathy jumped and landed on the side of her foot, then fell down. "Ow," she moaned, massaging her ankle. "You took the light away too soon."

Todd flashed the beam at her foot then in her face. "Is it sprained?"

Kathy squinted. "It's okay—and take that light away. You're blinding me."

Todd took his time climbing the rest of the hill and Kathy hobbled along. "Then you don't think there's really a ghost at the manor?"

"It's like a legend," Todd explained. "Jenny drowned and no one knew how, so everyone told everyone else what they thought happened. Put all that together and pass it down forever and Mike's got himself a whopper of a story. A real scary one that people with active imaginations believe. I like to hear him tell it, because someday I plan to use all his stories when I write my book."

"I don't know," Kathy said. "Until I find out who that woman is, I'm not doubting Mike. Besides, I was watching his face and it looked like he believed what he was saying."

"Maybe he's told it so many times he does believe it—but I don't. To me, seeing is believing, and I've never seen anything or anyone who isn't real."

"But what if you did?"

Todd shined his light up at the dark sky. "Everything's explainable," he said. "You just have to prove it. My dad was a scientist and he said so."

He walked on in silence and Kathy sensed he was feeling sad. "My aunt told me about your dad. I'm sorry he's dead." When he didn't reply, Kathy added, "I think you're lucky though, inheriting two sisters."

"Lucky?" he said, with a half-laugh. "How would you know?"

"Because I'm an only child and I wish I had two sisters. Even one would do."

"Well, I *was* an only child," he said. "And I wanted it to stay that way."

The manor loomed up before them, its tower silhouetted against the sky like an old castle. Todd took off running toward the root cellar mound. He stopped by the gravel pile first and picked up a handful of pebbles. "Grab some," he called back. "Let's see if we can hit the stars."

Kathy threw as high as she could and waited for Todd.

"Hey," he commented. "You've really got an arm on you. Do you play ball?"

"Nope. But I've got muscles. I swing on the bars at school and sometimes I use my mom's weights at home."

They took turns tossing until they were tired out, then dropped to the mound and laughed happily together. The night was warm. Todd lay on his back and rested his head on his crossed arms. He studied the sky. "Have you ever tried to find the planets? They look like bright stars. See, there's Venus over there—and Mars and Jupiter—and there's Saturn." He pointed them out and Kathy counted.

"What about the rest of them?" She traced her finger in the air. "There's Pluto over there."

"I don't think so," Todd said lazily. "You need a telescope to find Pluto and Neptune and Uranus. They're pretty dim. You don't need one to see

71

Mercury, though. Sometimes you can see it just after the sun sets. Other times it's visible just before the sun rises. The sky's not very dark then, but you'd have to be a good sky-watcher to find it."

Kathy was impressed. "Have you been studying the Solar System in school?"

"Sure. But I study at home too. I've got lots of books and a telescope. My dad was an astronomy professor at Sierra College."

"Todd—look," Kathy said excitedly. "A shooting star."

"A meteor falling toward Earth," he said matter-of-factly. "It's nothing to get hyped up about. It's just bits of rock and metal."

"I don't care what it is," she said. "It's beautiful— did you see the flashing tail?"

"Have you ever seen a meteor shower?" Todd asked. "Now that's something. I read that they're the remains of long-dead comets moving in streams across the Solar System."

"I saw Halley's comet," Kathy said. "Everyone did, but there was no shower."

"If you're still around here in August," he said, "we might see the Perseid shower."

Kathy recalled Mike's parting words about none of the Wicklows living at the manor being safe. "What do you mean if I'm still around?"

He glanced over at her. "If you're still here—at

Riversend." He raised up on his elbows. "If we come up here regularly and we're able to spot a comet some night—and we're the first ones to report it—we could name it after us. We could call it the Malone-Wicklow."

"Or the Kathy-Todd," she said brightly.

Todd looked at her curiously. "It's been said that comets often bring doom."

Kathy grew serious. "Then maybe we should keep a close watch. I don't want any surprises." Todd stretched out and she began to whistle.

"Wish I could whistle like that," Todd said enviously.

"It's easy." Kathy whistled louder. "It just takes practice."

Todd gave a sharp whistle through his teeth. "That's the only way I can do it."

From down by the river, Nugget brayed.

"And that's the way I call him," Todd said, grinning. Nugget brayed again. "That's the way he lets me know where he is."

Just then, there was a thumping noise beneath them. Kathy stared at Todd fearfully. "What was that?" she whispered.

"Rats in the cellar," he said, getting up and stomping on top of the mound. "They probably live down in that old hole."

Another thump answered his stomp and Todd

jumped. From behind him, Kathy reached out and grabbed his arm. "They must be rats with big fists," she said, trembling.

Todd banged on the side of the mound twice with his foot.

Two thumps hit back.

Kathy shrieked and ran. Todd caught up with her and grasped her hand. "It's just rats, I said."

"Yeah, well, if it's just rats, they can count. Come on. Let's get out of here."

Kathy shook free of his grip and headed for the back door. Todd took off down the hill. "I won't be around tomorrow or the next day," he called back. The beam from his flashlight bounced ahead of him like a ghostly ball.

"Why not?" Kathy hollered, suddenly feeling deserted.

"I'll be in Placerville with my mom."

She watched from the doorway until she couldn't see his light anymore, then gave a furtive glance toward the mound before she shut the door tightly behind her.

CHAPTER
9

"How was dinner?" asked Sharon, removing her glasses and setting them on the table along with her book. "Did you have a good time?"

"Dinner was great. Mike made mulligan stew and . . ." She hesitated, wondering if she should tell her aunt about Mike's ghost story, even though Todd had warned her not to.

Sharon leaned forward in her chair. "And what?" she asked expectantly.

Kathy limped over to the table and dropped into a chair. Now that the excitement about the rats was over, her foot hurt. She glanced over at her aunt, whose face was filled with concern. "Todd had a flashlight," she hurriedly explained, "but I still stumbled on a chuckhole." She gave a nervous giggle. "Clumsy me."

Sharon knelt down in front of Kathy. She lifted the injured foot and examined it. "It doesn't look swollen. Where does it hurt?"

"It's okay," Kathy said, pulling her foot away. "I'll soak it in the tub tonight. It'll be fine."

"What's wrong, Kathy?" asked Sharon. "You seem flustered. Are you positive everything went all right at Mike's? How did you get along with Todd?"

"Pretty good," Kathy said, drumming her fingers on the table. "He knows a lot about the stars and planets—the whole Solar System." She gazed up at the ceiling. "I like that stuff. But he's leaving tomorrow to go home." She sighed deeply. "Then I won't have anyone to talk to—I mean there's you," she added quickly.

"I know what you mean," said Sharon. "But don't worry. Todd's mother picks him up every Saturday morning and brings him back to the cabin on Sunday night."

Kathy's eyes lit up. "Great. We can search for the planets again, or comets."

"Summer nights in Riversend are perfect for sky watching," Sharon said. "We're far enough away from the city lights to have a brilliant display." She smiled to herself and nodded. "Seems Todd gets his interest in the universe from his

76

father. His dad and I gazed at the stars many summer nights when we were kids. He wanted to be an astronaut."

Kathy heard sadness in her aunt's voice. "Were you still friends when he died?"

"When I returned to open the manor, Mike told me what had happened. It had been years since I'd seen him, but it was a real shock."

If her aunt was shocked, Kathy thought, what had it been like for Todd? "Does Todd look like him?"

Sharon smiled wistfully as she nodded. "Especially when he wears that old straw hat. It belonged to his dad. I know Todd cherishes it, because he wears it most of the time."

It looked like her aunt was temporarily lost in memories, so mentioning the woman on the hill didn't seem like a good idea right now. But she had to know about the root cellar. "Are there rats around here?" she blurted out, getting Sharon's immediate attention.

Sharon shuddered. "I'm sure there are," she said. "Why? Did you see one?"

"We didn't see anything, but we heard a noise and Todd said it was rats."

"Down by the river, you mean," Sharon said with a positive nod.

Kathy shook her head hard. "No. Up here—over at the mound. It kind of scared me."

Sharon's eyes grew dark. "Describe what you heard."

"It was a thumping—loud." She waited, but her aunt was silent. "Aunt Sharon," she insisted. "Was it rats?"

Sharon reached for her book and clutched it with white knuckles. "Probably," she said in a strained voice. "Let me know if you hear it again." She stood up.

"Can we check it out tomorrow?" Kathy asked. "If it is rats, won't they get into your lemons?"

"I can't worry about lemons now," Sharon said, brushing the subject aside. "I've got three interviews for kitchen help tomorrow. Come on," she said tightly. "It's bedtime. I'll walk you to the stairs."

Kathy followed, wondering why her aunt was suddenly so upset. Was she so afraid of rats that she couldn't even talk about them? Or was it something else? When she reached the stairs, Kathy used her arms to pull herself up past the bottom step.

"Why did you do that?" Sharon asked.

Kathy turned quickly. "Do what?"

"Skip that bottom step?"

"There's an icky smell down there," Kathy said, making a face. "I don't want to step on it."

Sharon's face paled. It looked almost as white as the mystery woman's face when she had peered up

78

at Kathy on the balcony. No way would she mention the woman in the cloak now — or the ball of mist on the stair. She even regretted asking about the rats.

"Is it a musty smell like in the root cellar?" Sharon stammered.

Kathy nodded. "Can't you smell it? It gets really strong sometimes." Sharon looked like she might faint and Kathy started back down the stairs.

"No. Stay there," Sharon directed, holding up her hand. She stared down at the step. "Go to bed now." When Sharon looked up, Kathy could see fear shining in her eyes. "If you need me for any reason at all, yell and I'll be right up."

Kathy promised, then rushed to her room and locked the door behind her. Gypsy was waiting for her on the bed, and Kathy slipped down beside her on top of the comforter.

"Something is very wrong here," she said, rubbing Gypsy's head. "Maybe Aunt Sharon's already seen the ghost. Or maybe Mike's warned her about the banshee. Or maybe the banshee ghost is in the cellar." She leaned back on her pillow and Gypsy cuddled up on her chest.

"And how about you?" she said, staring into the cat's shrewd eyes. "What have you seen and heard?"

CHAPTER
10

Kathy couldn't tell exactly which noise had jarred her out of a deep sleep. She wasn't sure if it was the banging and rapping, the despairing sighs and sobs, or the clattering that seemed to come from the far corner of the room.

She lay still for a moment staring out into the dark. Then she ran her hand down over the comforter, searching for Gypsy's familiar form. But the cat was gone.

Surprised to find that she was still dressed and that she was lying on top of the covers instead of underneath them, she felt naked and unprotected without a blanket to pull up over her head.

A loud *poof!* from the fireplace made her jump.

The room instantly lit up and shadows seemed to leap off the walls and ceiling. She closed her eyes tightly, trying to blot out the strange events going on around her, but the harder she forced her eyes shut, the louder the noises got.

Her throat felt swollen. She had to swallow, but she knew if she tried, she would gag. Memories of Mike's tale about the banshee pounded through her mind, and she froze at the thought that the ghost might be after her and not Aunt Sharon.

She began to tremble. Her breath came in short gasps. Just when she was sure she would faint from terror, she felt a light comforting touch on the lower part of her arm.

"Aunt Sharon?" she cried, sitting up. But it wasn't Sharon standing next to the bed, it was the cloaked woman, shimmering in the shadows. She was gazing down and stroking Kathy's arm with her fingers. When Kathy found the courage to look up, she saw that the woman's eyes were filled with tears.

The woman swayed back and forth with her head bowed. Her cheeks were damp from crying. When she raised her head, the cuffed hood of her cloak fell back, revealing a cascade of dark hair that fell around her shoulders like a black cloud.

She remained at Kathy's side for a minute, then turned and glided across the room to the fireplace. Kathy watched, amazed, as she floated above the floor. No one can walk in the air, Kathy thought — except a ghost.

The woman hovered next to the hearth, holding out her hands in an effort to warm them by a fire that blazed away on an empty grate. Kathy spotted Gypsy on the floor. Her tail twitched as she stared up at the intruder.

The ghost turned and gave Kathy a long, sorrowful look. Concern flooded Kathy's heart, pushing the fear aside, as she watched the poor woman trying to warm herself. But her fear returned with a jolt when the balcony doors flew open and a silver whirlwind rushed over the railing and into the room.

It spun near Kathy's bed, then sprang to the fireplace, where it cut a zigzag through the phantom fire before depositing a thick coat of ash on the hearth. After circling the cloaked woman, the wind flew around a startled Gypsy, then whirled back through the doors and into the night.

The room became deathly still. Kathy grabbed her pillow and clutched it against her chest. The ghost stared at Kathy with desperate eyes, but Kathy tried to ignore her. When she beckoned for Kathy to come to her, Kathy didn't move. But when the woman tilted her head to the side in a pleading gesture, Kathy felt a great sadness, and she was unable to resist.

Standing unsteadily, Kathy wove her way to the

fireplace and stood next to Gypsy. The woman's eyes softened with gratitude. She leaned over and pointed her finger at the hearth. Five large letters appeared in the ashes: TOWER. The ghost gazed at Kathy, then looked at the word.

"Tower," Kathy said out loud, breaking the silence. Startled by her own voice, she stepped back into the shadows, stumbling over Gypsy. The cat yowled and Kathy reached down and pulled her up. The ghost pointed twice to the hearth, hesitated, then floated over to the closed door and passed through it.

"Wow, did you see that?" Kathy whispered to Gypsy. She rushed over and unlocked the door, then peered out. The shimmering ghost was at the end of the corridor waiting in the arched entrance to the tower. She lifted her hand and with a slow, sweeping motion beckoned Kathy to join her.

Kathy stepped out into the hall. The door slammed behind her. She felt for the knob and struggled to turn it, but it wouldn't move. Scared, she glanced down the hall for help. But the ghostly figure only swayed her head from side to side.

What did the ghost want? What was she trying to tell her? Was she here to do her harm, as Mike had said, or did she somehow need Kathy's help? Kathy's curiosity finally nudged her on. She started down the hall, hesitating at every door before continuing.

When Kathy reached the small landing inside the entrance to the tower, the woman welcomed her by brushing her arm again. This time Kathy could see that the pale fingers didn't touch her at all. The woman used them as a wand just above her skin, creating vibrations that made her feel calm.

Kathy managed a faint smile, and for a moment she was sure the ghost smiled back. Then, with a swish of her cloak, the woman moved swiftly up the circular stairs that hugged the tower wall.

Circular stairs! Kathy stared up. They were just like a picture she had drawn at school! Miss Collins had hung the drawing on the art board for Parent's Night.

Now what? She remembered her aunt's warning about the danger of going up the stairs. But what if Kathy were the mistress of the manor to have the visitations? Just like Mike said. Hadn't she already had message dreams? And sketched pictures of places and things she'd never seen before? Maybe the tower held a special message for her.

She squinted into the dark, trying to see the tower room, but she could only see as far as the large gap where the steps were missing. Inching her way to the edge of the landing, she looked down toward the ground floor, but it was way too dark to see. She shuddered. Her aunt was right— the gap was dangerous. What if she fell?

84

A lantern materialized on the first step. The ghost bent over and picked it up. She motioned for Kathy, then rose up one step at a time. When Kathy didn't follow, the ghost turned, her eyes filled with expectancy. A cold wind blew down through the tower, billowing the woman's cloak and lifting her hair like wings. *Come Katherine — come*, the wind echoed in Kathy's ears. *Come — see.*

Kathy placed her foot on the first step, then stopped. Her aunt had warned her not to go up. She rubbed Gypsy's neck. "What should I do?" she whispered. The cat glared at her through slitted eyes and moaned. Did that mean go or stay?

As the woman waited, the light from the lantern cast ominous shadows on the brick walls.

Should she follow her ancestor or obey her aunt?

The hall light clicked on. Quick footsteps headed her way. Kathy twirled around just in time to look into the shocked eyes of her aunt Sharon.

"Kathy," she cried, grabbing her arm and pulling her out into the hall. "What are you doing in there?"

Kathy was too startled to speak. All she could do was point to the circular steps.

"You were going up to the tower room?" Sharon's eyes filled with disbelief. "After I warned you — told you not to?"

Kathy turned and looked back, but the ghost had disappeared.

"You must have been sleepwalking," Sharon said as she guided Kathy back to her room. "I heard your door slam." She tugged at Kathy's shirt. "Why are you still dressed? I should never have left you alone up here."

Kathy was silent. She rubbed her eyes, not knowing where to begin.

When they reached the bedroom, Sharon turned the doorknob and it opened easily. Inside, she leaned against the closed door looking frazzled. She placed her hand against her chest as she sucked in a deep breath. Then she moved swiftly around the room, gathering up Kathy's gown and slippers. "You're coming downstairs and sleeping in my room," she said firmly. After an uneasy glance around the room, she rushed over, shut and locked the balcony doors, then went back to Kathy and took Gypsy from her arms.

"The cat stays here," she said, placing her on the bed. "I don't want to deal with her tonight. You can come up in the morning and let her out."

Sharon opened the door and checked the hall. Gypsy leaped from the bed and escaped between her legs, then raced for the landing. Kathy tried to push past Sharon to get her.

"Let her go," Sharon said, circling Kathy's wrist with her hand. "Nothing will happen to her—I promise you." She stopped, studied Kathy's face, and affectionately brushed her hair back. "It's going to be all right," she said, kissing her lightly on the forehead. "We'll talk about this in the morning."

CHAPTER
11

The next morning Kathy awoke to the sound of women's voices coming from the kitchen. She slipped out of bed and opened the door a crack. Aunt Sharon, sitting across the table from a blond woman, was asking her about her cooking experience. Kathy remembered about the interviews her aunt had scheduled for the day.

Relieved that she didn't have to explain about last night's events, at least not now, Kathy opened the door all the way. She waved brightly at the blond woman and grabbed an apple muffin from the counter.

Sharon turned just as Kathy reached the hall door. "Good morning," she said, smiling. "Sit down and have a glass of milk with that muffin."

Kathy had a hard time swallowing the huge bite of muffin she'd just taken. "I'll be back later," she mumbled. "I'm going up to get dressed."

Instead of climbing the stairs to her room, Kathy tiptoed past the kitchen and continued on down to the end of the hall. There must be a tower entrance here, she reasoned. But there wasn't. There was only a plastered, painted wall.

Sharon had said that a carpenter was coming. Would she have him build a wall like this at the end of the corridor upstairs? Kathy folded her arms and frowned. If that was the plan, and if Kathy wanted to get up to the tower room, then it would have to be soon. She nodded. Whatever the ghost wanted her to see, she had a strong feeling she needed to see it.

She walked back to the staircase and ran up. At the end of the second-floor corridor, she peered in at the circular stairway. The same stairs she had sketched in her tablet! Even in the daytime the light was dim, but at least now she could see up to the open entrance of the room.

Was that where the ghost stayed? Had that been Lora's room? Did Kathy draw the stairs because she was supposed to climb them? She stepped onto the landing and a shudder raced across her shoulder blades.

Leaning over the handrail, she looked down to

89

the stone floor below. To the right was a heavy wooden door that led outside. So that was the other way into the tower. Through the yard.

She felt someone watching her. Glancing around nervously, she tried her old trick for courage — whistling. But nothing came out except a squeak. Feeling helpless, she turned quickly and ran down the hall to her room. She immediately crossed to the fireplace. Most of the ashes from last night were gone. Only the letter R from the word TOWER remained, proof that she hadn't been dreaming or sleepwalking.

Gypsy pounced out of nowhere and landed on the hearth in front of her. The cat flicked her tail back and forth, erasing the only evidence Kathy had. "Gypsy," Kathy said, astonished. "Look what you've done." She scooted the cat out into the hall. If she ever decided to tell her aunt or Todd about this, they'd never believe her now.

Stomping over to the balcony doors, she unlocked them and pushed them open. She gazed toward the river. Mike would believe her, but she had one important stop to make before she went down to see him.

After she got dressed, she packed up a tote bag with her sketchbook, colored pencils, and charcoal sticks. Hurrying down the stairs, she left by the front door, closing it softly behind her. Gypsy was sprawled on the veranda. Kathy stared thoughtfully at her, then kneeled down. "I'm sorry," she said. "I know you didn't erase that letter on purpose." She hesitated a moment. "Did you?"

Gypsy winked and began to lick the soft inward curve of her paw. Kathy jumped up. "There's something I'd really like to know, though. Did you go with her to the tower room last night?"

The cat's eyes flickered and her whiskers twitched.

"Don't want to talk about it, huh?" Kathy gave her a rub. "Don't blame you. I don't either." She looked back at the front door. "But I bet I'll have to."

She left the cat basking in the sun and walked around to the side of the house. Cutting a path through the tall grass, she reached the entrance to the tower. Weeds sprouted as high as the rusty handle of the arched wooden door where a large shiny padlock hung down. Kathy twisted the lock.

There was no getting through that door. And there was no other entrance to the tower except upstairs, and that would soon be gone. She headed down the road, munching on the rest of the apple muffin. A short distance from the front of the house, she stopped and looked up at the tower windows. Was someone watching her? The morning sun hit the two windows, blinding her. She shaded her eyes with her hand and squinted, but she couldn't see what was on the other side of the glass.

Moving on, she soon came to the Wicklow grave-yard. It was Jenny's grave she had come to find. But the old yard looked creepy with its high weeds and leaning tombstones. It needed caretaking. Weeding and gardening had never interested Kathy, but now she felt a responsibility to her ancestors. She felt a tie to Jenny's portrait and had possibly met the ghost of Lora. When Todd came back, maybe she would ask him to help her clean up the graveyard.

Kathy tried to enter, but the metal gate wouldn't open. The weeds had tangled around it so tightly it wouldn't budge. She pushed and pulled then finally gave up.

The only way to get in was to climb over. She dropped her tote bag to the other side. Boosting herself up, she caught her shorts on a metal picket, ripping the inside seam.

"Rats," she cried, checking the damage. Then she giggled nervously. Saying *rats* brought back thoughts of the thumpings from the cellar. Her eyes searched the ground around her feet. When she was sure the ground was clear of rodents, she picked up her tote and moved on, watching out for scurrying feet or dragging tails.

She spotted a dirt line that was once a path and quickly picked her way along. A low rumble of thunder from the other side of the mountains made her stop and look up. Dark clouds were forming around the peaks.

Kathy walked on until the path ended at the foot of a cracked headstone. She stepped to the side to pass. As she did, she saw someone kneeling inside a plot where three evenly spaced markers stood next to an unmarked space at the end. As Kathy got closer, she could see that it was a woman—and she was wearing a cloak. A wind blew up and a low-pitched crying broke out over Kathy's head, then faded away behind her.

Kathy hopped over to get a better view, tripping on an old board jutting up from the grass. When she looked back, the woman was gone.

Lora, she thought. She wanted me here. That's why I came. But why? Kathy crossed to the plot and stood next to the low railing. The weeds inside the fence had been pulled and there were fresh flowers on the three marked graves. One long-stemmed pink rose rested on the unmarked space. Kathy searched the area for Lora. She could feel her, but she couldn't see her.

Lora must have come to pay tribute to her family. Kathy stared down at the rose. That must be the plot Lora's family had reserved for her.

She stepped over the fence, picked up the rose, and smelled it. Drops of moisture on the fragile petals reminded her of tears. Carefully returning

the rose to the unmarked space, she stepped back
and read the headstones.

James Wicklow, banker
A native of Ireland
Died 1859

Arabella, wife of James Wicklow
Died 1856

Jenny, beloved daughter of James
and Arabella Wicklow
Died 1860
As you are now, so once was I
As I am now, so you must be

Was the message at the bottom of Jenny's headstone chiseled there for Lora to read? Poor Jenny,
Kathy thought sadly. Drowned, then washed away
down the cold river. Her eyes rested on the unmarked
plot. "And Lora," she said out loud, casting her
words to the wind. "I wonder where you're buried."

Slowly she made her way back to the gate and
tried it again. It was still stuck. Above her the
quickly gathering clouds threatened rain. As she
climbed over the fence, the wind whispered in her
ears, *Katherine— help me. Katherine— the tower—
message.*

Just as she suspected! *Message!* That word made
her feel uneasy. If she gave in to Lora's plea and
tried to get up to the tower room, Aunt Sharon
would be very angry with her. And if she didn't?

When she got to the manor, she walked past the tower, stretching her neck to see up to the windows. One window at the back of the tower looked out over the hill. If a person was standing up there, Kathy reasoned, she would have a panoramic view of Riversend. She peeked around, searching for her aunt. The backyard was empty except for a bike propped next to the door.

Must belong to the blond woman, Kathy thought. Good! Her aunt was still busy.

The clouds had passed, and the sun beat down on Kathy's head. Dragging her feet, she stumbled over the unfinished walkway that led to the root cellar. When she reached the crest of the hill, she searched the riverbank for Mike. He still wasn't there. Disappointed, she plopped on a yard chair next to a white metal table with a faded umbrella rising up from the center. She looked up at the tower, then reached for her art supplies and started to draw.

First she made a rough sketch of the rear of the manor; then she added the tower with the witch-hat roof. As she worked, she whistled. Once she was sure she saw a woman in the window wearing a white cap. But when Kathy blinked, the face was gone.

Suddenly, the picture of the manor was ripped from her tablet and tossed to the ground. One at a time, her colored pencils were forced between her fingers and held there as they flew across the heavy art paper, sketching faster than Kathy had ever done before.

Too shocked to move or speak, Kathy just stared at her hand. If she wasn't making the pencils move, then who was?

"Hungry?" a voice called from behind her. The paper and pencils dropped from Kathy's hands. She twisted around to see her aunt coming towards her with a tray of sandwiches and a pitcher of lemonade. Sharon set the tray on the table and bent over to pick up the picture. She gasped and turned angry eyes on Kathy.

"You did go to the tower!" she cried. "And after I warned you." Dropping into the chair next to Kathy, she leaned her head on her hand.

"I didn't," Kathy stammered. "I only went to the landing."

Sharon looked up. Her eyes were filled with fear and disappointment. "Kathy, stop it. Don't lie to me." She rattled the paper against the tabletop. "You know as well as I do what this is."

Kathy pressed her shoulders against the back of the chair and made a face. "But I didn't draw that."

Sharon's face reddened. Holding the picture up to Kathy's face, she cried, "Look at this. Do you expect me to believe you? You were drawing on this paper not more than two minutes ago. The only way you could have drawn this is if you had gone to the tower room."

Sharon stood and paced in front of the table, glancing up at the tower window. "I should have walled off that landing before you got here," she said, more to herself than to Kathy. "But with all I've had to do . . ." She shook her head. "How did you get past that gap in the stairs?"

Kathy wanted to run, to jump up and get as far away from her aunt as she could. But she knew that wouldn't work. She'd have to face her sometime. "I didn't go to the tower room," she repeated. "And I didn't draw this picture." She turned her face away, preparing herself for her aunt's angry outburst. But instead Sharon started to cry. It was a frustrated crying that made Kathy feel awful.

"You won't be in trouble," Sharon pleaded, her eyes looking a little like Lora's. "Just tell me the truth—please."

"I am," Kathy said slowly. "I'm not lying."

Sharon stared at her for a long while, then stood up. "I can't accept that, Kathy," she said stiffly. Then her voice quavered. "When you're ready to tell me what happened, I'll be waiting for you in the kitchen."

Sharon went in the house and Kathy picked up the picture and stared at the artwork. Her aunt must be crazy if she thought she could draw a woman's face like that. This drawing was beautiful.

She looked helplessly down to the river. "Mike, where are you?"

CHAPTER
12

Kathy gulped her lemonade while she tried to figure out what to do. Should she go in and tell her aunt everything from the beginning? About the cloaked woman on the hill? Mike's banshee story? The visit from the ghost in her room last night?

What about Lora at the family plot?

If Sharon didn't believe her when she said she hadn't been to the tower and she hadn't drawn the picture, why would she believe her story about the ghost?

Sharon was definitely scared about something. That was why Kathy wanted to talk to Mike. If he had warned Sharon about the banshee, maybe that's why she was acting so nervous.

Kathy shaded her eyes and looked up. The woman in the white cap was looking down at her. Her head nodded rhythmically, up and down, up and down. Why was she nodding? What did it mean? You got me into this, Kathy thought angrily, as she stared back without blinking. Now why don't you help me get out?

The woman kept right on nodding. Did the nodding mean that everything would be all right? Kathy hoped so. But that didn't help her right now. The longer she stared up at the woman's face, the more relaxed she became. Soon she was leaning back and stretching her arms.

The back door swung open and Sharon and a new woman stepped out. This one had dark hair. The other one must have left by the front door. As the two women talked, Kathy took advantage of the moment. She reached for her tote, quickly rolled up the picture, and shoved it in the bag. Then she grabbed a sandwich from the plate, turned, and went down the hill. If she couldn't find Mike, she would sit on a big rock and sketch—and think.

She plodded down the hill. Halfway, she stopped and opened the raisin bread sandwich and looked inside. It was filled with chopped nuts mixed with cream cheese. She closed it and took a big bite. Umm—good!

The food at the manor was different from what

her mother fixed at home. That was probably why she'd heard her mother call her aunt weird. At least she hoped that was the reason.

Nearing the river, she heard Nugget braying down at the cabin. Making a sharp turn, she ran toward Mike's.

"Gosh darn it." She could hear Mike's cracked voice hollering out. "You stubborn old mule."

Nugget, loaded down with canvas bags, shovels, buckets, pans, and a pick, stood out in front of the cabin with a banjo tied to his side. His bridle was strapped securely across his nose, and every time Mike yelled, Nugget's tail twitched.

"Why are you yelling?" Kathy called. "You're hurting his feelings."

Mike's head jerked around at the sound of Kathy's voice. His angry eyes softened when he saw who it was. "Missy," he said with relief. "Maybe you can talk some sense into this ornery critter." A flicker of annoyance crossed his face. "And it's not Nugget's feelings you should be concerned about, it's mine, and a lot of other disappointed folks. It's Saturday and we're expected in town. Usually this fella can't wait to get going, but now he won't budge."

Kathy set her tote down and went over to Nugget. She put her arms around his thick neck and gave him a kiss on his face. "He probably just wants to stay here today," she said, petting the spot between

100

his eyes. "It's awfully hot, you know." Nugget stood very still and let Kathy rub her face against his.

"If he'd done what he was supposed to, we'd have been there before it got hot," Mike grumbled. "I can't figure what got into him."

"Maybe he misses Todd," Kathy said.

The old man scratched his head up under his hat. "That's not likely. The boy's been gone every Saturday for the last month. Nope. It's got to be something else."

"Maybe he needs a vacation."

"That could be. You might have struck it, Missy. Who knows what goes on in that old boy's head." He sat down on the edge of the cabin step, then squinted at Kathy and Nugget. "You two look like old pals. It could be that he didn't want to go to town without you."

Kathy looked pleased. "Do you really think so? If I'd known you were going, I would have asked my aunt for permission, but Todd said you'd be panning for gold all day."

Mike leaned his head back and scanned the sky. "Todd wasn't telling tales. There's a storm brewing. We don't usually head out when it's darkening up, but the weather can't seem to make up its mind. First it's sunny, then it's cloudy." He angled a look at the burro. "Sometimes animals know better than humans what's going on with the elements. Guess the old boy didn't want to take a chance. He hates thunder and lightning."

He pushed himself up from the step. "Since you're here, how about the three of us going upstream? I'll show you how to get yourself some gold."

Kathy's eyes widened. "Really? I'd love to." She picked up her bag and grabbed Nugget's rope.

"Hold on there a minute," Mike ordered. He looked down at his red shirt. "I can't go up the river in this—it's my town shirt." He went in the cabin. When he returned, it looked to Kathy as if he was wearing the same shirt.

"Now," he said, rolling up his sleeves. "Let's go."

Kathy led Nugget toward the riverbank, following close behind Mike, whose denim pants were tucked into his high boots. As he trudged along, he kicked up small clouds of dust that made Kathy sneeze. Occasionally he would stop, lean over, and spit on the dirt.

"You and the boy getting along any better?" he asked over his shoulder.

"Todd?" Kathy shrugged. "I guess so. When will he be back?"

Mike turned around and grinned. "Tomorrow— late. Why? Do you miss him?"

Kathy blushed. "Well, I don't have any sisters or brothers, and he's the only other kid around here."

They walked along in silence, then Mike said, "You have to have patience with that boy. He's a strange one. He doesn't believe in anything he can't see. He'll spend hours gazing up at the stars and other times he can't see past the tip of his nose."

Doesn't believe— doesn't believe. The words throbbed through Kathy's thoughts, bringing back the problem with her aunt. "Mike . . ."

Mike cupped his ear with his hand. "Come on up here, so I can hear you."

Pulling Nugget along with her, she caught up with Mike, then strode along with him, keeping her eyes on the ground. "I've got a problem," she said.

Mike gave her a sidelong look. "I could tell that as soon as I saw you down by the cabin." He waited but she didn't continue. "You've seen that banshee again, haven't you?"

Kathy looked up and vigorously shook her head. "I don't think the ghost is a banshee. I think it's Lora."

Mike frowned. "What makes you think she's not a banshee?"

Kathy filled him in on what had happened since last night. She talked about the thumpings in the cellar and the ghost hovering above the floor in her bedroom, about her aunt finding her on the tower landing, and about seeing Lora at the graveyard. She stopped walking and let Nugget's rope drop while she dug into her tote for the picture. Suddenly free, Nugget took off at a trot, his pack clanking against his sides.

Mike let out a shrill whistle, but Nugget ignored him and kept on going. "Gosh-darned stubborn . . ." Mike was after him, stiffly running until he caught up with him. When he brought the burro back, Mike was panting and his face was as red as his shirt. "He can sure travel when he wants to," Mike said, shooting Nugget a dark look.

Kathy tried not to laugh, but she couldn't help it. Nugget looked like he was having such a good time. "Can you teach me to whistle like that?" She giggled, forgetting for the moment about her problems.

"I taught Todd and his daddy and his daddy before him," Mike said, letting out another shrill sound. "If I can still whistle without my teeth, you can sure learn to do it with a full set." He forced his lips into a thin line and opened his mouth just a sliver. "You put your tongue here and . . ." His voice trailed off as the picture in Kathy's hand unrolled. "So." He nodded. "You've been up to the tower room." Carefully lifting the paper from Kathy's hand, he studied the woman's face. "She's a beauty, isn't she?"

Kathy felt a tightening in her stomach. "It's Lora, isn't it?"

"You betcha," Mike said admiringly. "They don't come like that anymore. No wonder my grandpappy was in love with her." He leaned his head to the right, then gazed at the picture head-on. He breathed a deep sigh and handed it back. "What did you think of the tower room?"

"I haven't been up there. That's my problem. My aunt thinks I have when she told me not to. She thinks I drew this."

Mike studied Kathy's face. "Lora's portrait hangs in that tower room. If you haven't been up there, then who—"

"I think Lora did," Kathy interrupted. "It was my paper and pencils, but my hand moved without me." She fought back tears that were threatening to spill over.

"Don't fret now," Mike said, his voice gentle. "That Lora's capable of anything."

"I know that now," Kathy said. "And I know she's trying to tell me something, but what?"

Mike rubbed his chin. "Let me ponder this for a while. We'll talk about it later. Right now we're going to . . . look! There's the spot right over there." He pointed to a bend in the river where a shallow pond was filled with black dirt and rocks. He dug around in Nugget's pack and removed two shallow pans with sloping sides.

"Here, Missy. Take this." He handed her one. "There's not a trouble in this world that panning won't cure. Let's you and me go find us some gold."

He waded through the shallow water and squatted

105

next to a rock barrier. First he filled his pan with gravel and dirt, then he began washing it by holding the pan under the water. "This is a sandbar," he said, motioning for her to come next to him. "See the black sand?"

Kathy eyed the water. "If I come over there I'll get my shoes wet."

"So what?" Mike grunted. "They're tennis shoes, aren't they? They'll dry. Come on—but first, tie Nugget's rope to that tree."

She secured Nugget, then picked her way over. When she reached Mike, she peered over his shoulder. "Is this where the gold is?"

Mike nodded. "Whenever you see sand this color, you know there's gold around. It's just a matter of panning it out." He rotated his pan gently and tilted it slightly to let the loose dirt wash out. He checked to see if Kathy was watching, then scooped up more dirt. This time he stirred it with his fingers, picking out the larger pebbles and gravel. Then he worked the pan, spilling the lighter matter over the side.

Kathy crouched down beside him. "Where does the gold come from?"

"From the rocks. The river washes it out from the crevices."

She peered into the pan. "I don't see any."

"Hold your horses," Mike scolded. "You young ones have to learn patience. There's plenty of gold here, or near here. You'll see it soon enough. When we get it, it'll sink to the bottom of the pan. It's heavier than sand."

Kathy shaded her face from the sun. "It's hot out here," she complained. "I don't see anything in there but dirt."

"Go on over to Nugget and get that old straw hat hanging on the pack," Mike directed.

Kathy splashed back, found the hat, and put it on. "This is just like Todd's," she giggled.

"Look again, Missy," Mike said, squinting over at her. "There's holes in that one for ears. That's Nugget's hat. He wears it for the kids in town."

Kathy took it off and put it on Nugget, gently pulling his ears through the slots.

"Come on. Let's hit pay dirt," Mike called.

Taking the hat off Nugget, she put it on her head. Mike motioned for her to sit on a rock. "We'll get flakes today," he promised. "If you stay around these parts long enough, I guarantee you'll go back to the city with a nugget."

Kathy hunched her shoulders with excitement. "How big?"

Mike searched through his pants pocket. He pulled out a rough lump the size of a blackberry. "I found this one on the other side of those rocks. When you see rough edges like this, it means it's traveled a short distance down the river. That's why my claim is upstream." He handed it to her and Kathy held it between her thumb and finger, turning it from side to side, letting the sun dance off its edges.

"The farther the gold is washed down the river," he continued, "the smoother the nugget. If it gets washed down a long way, it turns to flakes, then finally to dust."

"Wow," Kathy said, impressed. "This is a beauty."

Mike helped her fill, wash, rotate, and tilt her pan. When the water uncovered an even layer of fine, dark, grainy sand, Mike let go. "Keep on sloshing now until the sand's nearly gone."

She nodded and followed his instructions. "Now what?" she asked, gripping the sides of the pan.

"That's it," Mike said, tossing down his hat. "Holler bonanza!"

"Bonanza?"

"That's right," Mike chuckled. "You've had a stroke of fortune, that's what bonanza means. Just a little one, I admit, but it's a stroke." He pointed and Kathy could see flashes of yellow glinting in the sun.

"It's gold," she yelled, almost dropping her pan.

Mike made a dash to balance it. "If you're going to be a miner, you don't want to lose your findings." Kathy let go, then did a little dance through the water. "I found gold," she repeated over and over. "I'm rich."

Kathy settled down as Mike poured what was left in the pan into a bottle of water. "It goes into a vial back at the cabin. Then you can take it home." As he twisted the cap shut, he turned and studied her. "I've been giving a lot of thought to your dilemma," he said somberly. "To your problem concerning the ghost."

The thrill of finding gold faded as Kathy thought about facing her aunt. She started to ask Mike what she could do when suddenly she felt a presence behind her. Looking into the water, she could clearly see the reflection of Lora's face just above the crown of her hat. She jerked around to tell Mike to look, but when she did, Lora was gone.

"I can't tell you exactly what to do," Mike was saying as he stirred the water with his fingers. "But I do think you should sit down and have a serious talk with Miss Sharon."

"Why? She won't believe me," Kathy insisted. "I think she's scared. She doesn't want to believe that all this stuff is going on."

"Well, she's known all about 'this stuff' since she was your age," Mike said. "I was the one who told her."

Kathy sat down on a boulder, placed her elbows on her knees, and supported her chin. That might explain it. "Has my aunt ever seen the ghost?" she asked.

109

"I believe she has," Mike said, gazing out over the river. "But she'd never admit to it. There was always something in that girl's eyes that made me think so."

"Mike, I'm not afraid of Lora's ghost," Kathy stated. "And no matter what you say, I don't think she's here to hurt anyone."

"You can believe what you like," Mike said, shaking his head. "But be careful what you do. Ghosts can be dangerous. Particularly if you have something that belongs to them."

Kathy jumped up. "Like what?"

"I don't know what," Mike said. "All I know is, that ghost wouldn't be hounding you without a good reason. When she was alive, Lora was a strong-minded woman. There's nothing to say that she's any different now that she's dead."

Kathy motioned over her shoulder. "Well, she's here right now and she hasn't done anything bad."

Mike struggled to his feet. "That banshee's here?" His eyes sparkled with excitement. "Where?"

"I saw her behind me," Kathy said as she waded over to the bank. "And she's no banshee. I think you're mean saying so."

Mike watched as she gathered up her things. "Are you leaving? We haven't even got a good start here yet."

"I'm going home," Kathy said, trying not to sound

rude, but somehow knowing she did. She didn't want to stay and hear bad stories about Lora. "Thanks for teaching me how to pan," she said.

"Missy. Don't do anything rash now," Mike warned. "That ghost is not one to mess with. If you're not careful, she'll lure you to the tower room and—"

"Don't, Mike," Kathy said, turning abruptly.

As she walked away, she left Mike staring after her with a puzzled frown on his face.

CHAPTER
13

Kathy had reached the top of the hill when she remembered she was still wearing Nugget's hat. She turned around to take it back when voices from the direction of the mound distracted her. She twirled back around and saw her aunt and a tall man lifting boxes from the back of a pickup truck. The door to the root cellar was open. Each time her aunt removed a box from the truck, the man ducked down the steps with it.

Kathy ran over and looked into the back of the truck. "Hi," she greeted her aunt enthusiastically. "Can I help?"

Sharon jumped at the sound of her voice. "Kathy," she said, relieved. "Sure. Give us a hand." She moved over to let Kathy grab one side of a crate. "I'm stocking up for the summer. I ordered all this when I was in Placerville yesterday."

The man poked his head out through the cellar door. "Tom, this is my niece, Kathy," Sharon said. "She's staying with me." She added softly, "For a while."

For a while. What did that mean? Was her aunt planning to send her home because she thought she had lied? Kathy felt helpless, then sad, because she didn't want to go home. Not yet. She wanted to stay here and get up to the tower room to find out what Lora was trying to tell her. No matter what Mike said.

Kathy and her aunt unloaded a crate of carrots, sweet potatoes, onions, and turnips for Tom to pick up. The last box contained yellow onions and the biggest bulbs of garlic Kathy had ever seen. "Did you grow these veggies?" Kathy asked Tom.

"Some of them," he replied, reaching for another crate. "But most of them are from the farmer's market in Placerville."

Kathy crouched down and peered into the cellar. "Do you see any rats down there?"

Tom's voice was muffled. "No." His face appeared at the opening and Kathy leaned back. "Why?" he asked. "Have you seen one?"

"No," she admitted. "But I think I heard one."

"Was it gnawing?" Tom glanced back in the hole.

"Nope. It was thumping."

Tom looked puzzled. "I've never heard of rats that thump. Have you, Sharon?"

Sharon looked distracted. "Really, you two. I have no idea what rats do. And I'm too busy to care."

Kathy felt uncomfortable. She shouldn't have mentioned the rats. It seemed to make her aunt nervous.

After the crates were all moved into the cellar, Tom came out. His face was streaked with dirt and sweat. "You should be set for a while, Sharon," he said, circling the mound, kicking at the sides with his boot. "You've got a weak spot right here, though." He motioned to the side where the unfinished path from the manor led to the mound. "I noticed it from the inside. It'll probably be okay for now, but you better reinforce it before the rains start."

Wow! That was the exact spot where Todd had kicked last night—the spot where they'd heard the thumping. While Sharon and Tom discussed how to repair it, Kathy peered down into the dimly lit hole. The crates were neatly stacked as far as she could see, but beyond that it was dark.

Sharon paid Tom, waved goodbye, then turned to Kathy. "Your parents called. Where were you?"

"They did?" Kathy said, disappointed. "Darn."

"They'll call back. I said you were probably down

at the river. Was I right?" She started toward the house.

Kathy tagged after her, dragging her tote, dreading the questions she might be asked once they were inside. "I was with Mike," she said slowly. Then her enthusiasm took over. "And guess what? I learned how to pan—and I found gold!" She ran alongside her aunt and looked up at her.

Sharon's face came alive with a smile. "Congratulations! Where is it?"

Kathy kept the tote with the picture of Lora behind her. "I don't have it now, but Mike's putting it in a vial. Then I can bring it home."

"You really look like a country girl now," Sharon said, observing the hat and Kathy's clothes, which were wet and splotched with dirt. She laughed and tugged at Kathy's shorts. "How did that happen?"

"I snagged it," Kathy said. "Aren't I clumsy?"

"That's Nugget's hat, isn't it?" said Sharon, touching the brim.

Kathy's eyes rolled as she shrugged. "I forgot to give it back."

"You can return it tomorrow when you pick up your gold." Sharon held open the kitchen door. "Kathy, about tomorrow. I'm delivering homemade cookies to the Sunday school in the morning. They're having a little celebration. If you want to come along, it's all right."

115

Her aunt would be gone in the morning. Kathy's mind whirred with the new information. She'd be alone in the house. That could be her chance to get up to the tower room before the carpenter came.

Kathy dragged her feet as she entered the house. "I don't think so," she said, making a face. "I don't know those kids in town. I'd feel like a stranger."

"I can understand that," Sharon said. "But if you change your mind, I'm leaving at nine." She went to the refrigerator, took out a covered dish, and turned on the oven. "We have to talk, Kathy." She turned around to face her. "But it's been a hectic day. When I get home from church tomorrow, let's plan to spend some time together. I'd like to straighten out what happened this afternoon." She forced a small smile. Kathy returned it.

Later, Sharon picked at her dinner, but Kathy ate hers up. "I'll do the dishes and box the cookies," Kathy offered. "I'm not tired."

Sharon eyed her curiously. "You're not? That would be a big help." She covered her mouth with her fingers as she yawned. "I could use a hot bath."

Kathy hurried to clear the table. Lora's ghost might visit her again tonight, and she didn't want to miss her.

Sharon stood uncertainly at the door. "All right then, honey. See you in the morning."

Kathy waited until almost eleven, but Lora didn't

116

show up. She propped herself up in bed while she sketched from memory the scene at the river when she had learned to pan. Then she read two chapters from her book, *Down a Dark Hall* by Lois Duncan. When her eyes were too heavy to read any more, she reached over with a sigh and turned off the lamp next to her bed.

The moonlight cast eerie shadows on the walls until the high clouds moved in front of the moon and blotted out the light. When the clouds passed, the shadows were there again.

She'd told Mike that she wasn't afraid of Lora, and that was the truth. But Kathy had to admit that she was scared sometimes by the weird things that happened when Lora appeared, like the fire in the empty grate, the silver whirlwind that swept through her room, and the strange winds that called her name. And those thumpings at the mound.

Switching the lamp on, she sat up against her pillow. Gypsy wasn't with her tonight and Kathy missed her. There'd been no sign of her since this morning on the veranda. Was she with Lora? Up in the tower room? Maybe she was prowling around the root cellar sniffing for rats.

She shivered at the thought of the dark hole at night. Turning off the light, she scrunched down under the covers. She must have dozed off, because the next thing she knew, she was opening her eyes to the sound of loud voices.

"You will not."

"I will do as I please."

"Do not try to stop me."

Kathy lay still in the dark, trying to figure out if it was her aunt arguing with someone downstairs. She listened closely. It wasn't her aunt's voice. The arguing sounded like two women and a man. She tiptoed to the door and listened. The voices stopped. Had she been dreaming?

She climbed back into bed and the talking started up again. A few words came through clearly, like *inheritance* and *dowry*, but most of what was said was muffled. Racing to the door, Kathy opened it. The voices stopped.

Crossing to the fireplace, she sat down on the hearth. The voices came through the wall. They all talked at once. Should she call out? Ask who they were—where they were?—try to find out what they were arguing about? She shuddered at the bad feelings that filled the room. Twisting the pocket on her nightgown, she thought the situation over.

If one of the voices was Lora's, then it might be safe to ask. But there was no way to tell. If Lora wasn't part of the clamor, and Kathy interfered, then she might be in for some real trouble.

She went back to bed and pulled the covers over

her head, but that didn't keep out the noise. Tossing to her right, then her left, she finally flopped over on her stomach, pressing the pillow over her ears. When the voices didn't stop, she threw back the covers, sat up in bed, and yelled "Stop it!"

The arguing ceased. The room became deathly still. Kathy waited. When nothing happened, she smiled self-consciously, scooted under the covers, and went to sleep.

Clink. Ping. Sounds against the glass on the balcony doors roused her. Turning over sleepily, she faced outside. The clouds had passed from the sky and the moon cast enough glow for her to make out the limb of the oak tree bouncing up and down.

Ping. Clink.

"Kathy," a voice called out in a hoarse whisper. Kathy's heart did a flip-flop. The limb of the tree creaked as jean-clad legs slid down closer to the balcony railing. A head appeared from under a clump of leaves.

It was Todd. His face twisted as he cried out hoarsely, "Kathy."

She jumped up and threw open the doors. "Todd," she said. "What are you doing in the tree?" She stepped out on the balcony barefoot, then hopped in pain as pieces of gravel stuck to the soles of her feet.

"I had to toss them at the window," Todd said before Kathy had time to complain. "It took forever to wake you up. Help me get down. My shirt's caught between those branches behind me and I can't reach it."

Kathy forgot about her feet. She pulled up a chair, climbed up on the railing, and balanced herself by holding onto the lower part of the branch. "Hold still," she ordered as Todd bounced around. "You're going to make me fall."

"Never mind," Todd said impatiently. "Just pull on me. Grab my arm."

Kathy didn't make a move until she had checked things out. It wasn't safe for her to climb on the branch to release him. He might bounce her off. And if she pulled on him hard, he might fall the wrong way and hit the ground.

"Hurry," he said, trying to whisper. "Just do it."

She grabbed hold of the front of his shirt and gave a yank. There was a loud ripping noise and Todd came sliding forward, sending the two of them tumbling. They knocked over the chair and landed side by side on the balcony floor.

"Well, if that didn't wake my aunt, nothing will," Kathy grumbled, jumping up.

Todd stood up, stretching to feel his back. "Now look what you've done—my shirt's torn. What'll I tell Mike?"

Kathy smoothed out her gown. "Mike?" she said, surprised. "What about me—and my aunt?" She glanced over at the hall door. "What if she heard us fall and she's on her way up here? Why are you here, anyway?"

Todd straightened the chair, then sat in it. "My mom's going to a wedding tomorrow. They all are. I didn't want to go, so she brought me back early."

Kathy crossed her arms. "So?"

Todd propped his feet on the railing. "I couldn't sleep. When I was in Placerville, I found something in one of my dad's—in one of *my*—astronomy books and I brought it for you to read." He teetered on the back legs of the chair. "Are you interested?"

Kathy was listening for her aunt. "Astronomy? Big deal!" She narrowed her eyes. "Does Mike know you're here?"

"Heck no. Are you crazy?" He held his watch to his eyes. "It's almost two-thirty."

Kathy tried to sound uninterested. "Well, where is it, this thing you want me to read?" She watched as he dug into his pants pocket.

"Have you ever heard of Flammarion?" Todd asked.

Kathy leaned casually against the door frame. "No, what is it?"

"You mean *who* is it." He stood and backed up to the railing, boosted himself up, then dangled his legs.

"Shh," Kathy cautioned. "Don't talk so loud. My aunt's room is right below us." She tiptoed over, leaned against the railing, and looked down. "Who's Flammarion?"

"He's a French astronomer," Todd said. "I mean he *was* an astronomer. He's dead now."

Kathy started for the door. "Big deal," she repeated. "Why should I care about a dead astronomer?"

"Because," Todd said. "He made maps of Mars, did balloon ascensions, studied double and multiple stars—"

Before he could finish, Kathy waved her hand in front of her face and gave a bored yawn.

"And because," Todd continued, "he published books on psychic research."

"You mean he saw things?" Kathy asked, getting interested. "Could he read people's minds? I didn't think you believed in stuff like that."

"I didn't say I believed." Todd sniffed. "I brought this back because you do. He doesn't say anything about mind reading, but he does write about haunted houses. He wrote that some houses might have some sort of memory of the people who lived in them."

Kathy plopped down on the chair. "He did?"

"Yep. See, I made a copy from the book."

She reached for the paper, but Todd whisked it away. "Turn on a light and we'll both read it."

Kathy stepped inside and Todd followed. She

122

switched on the lamp and they sat on the floor poring over the astronomer's words.

Houses might have some sort of memory, not a memory like a mind's memory, of course, but it would operate that way. The walls and floors and ceilings would be affected by nervous force—and this force once absorbed, like an impression in the mind, would be hidden most of the time, but could be called up upon occasion just as a memory may be called up.

Kathy didn't pretend to understand all of it, but the words *called up* caught her attention. She reread the last sentence. "Todd," she exclaimed, getting up on her knees and grabbing the front of his shirt. "My whistling! It's my whistling."

Todd shrugged her off. "What's that got to do with anything?"

"When I whistle I usually hear or see something." She got up and paced around the room. "I've seen things when I haven't whistled too, but when I do, I see Lora or something weird happens, like the thumping over on the mound."

"That again?" Todd winced. "I told you that was rats."

Kathy could have explained about how Tom, the vegetable man, had never heard of rats that thump, but she had more important matters to think about now.

"I've got to get back," Todd said.

"Wait," Kathy pleaded, blocking the door. "I need your help."

"Yeah? Like how?"

"My aunt's going to church in the morning," she said quickly before she lost her nerve. "And I want to go up to the tower room. I need you to stand outside by the door and let me know when she drives up."

He squinted suspiciously. "Why go when your aunt's not home? What's up there?"

"Never mind," Kathy said. "I'll tell you tomorrow — will you do it?"

Todd grinned slyly. "For a price. What's it worth?"

The jerk! Kathy thought a moment. "I'll finish the last walkway to the root cellar by myself. I'll fill it with gravel, but you'll still get paid." She nodded in a businesslike manner.

But Todd wasn't buying. He raised one eyebrow. "How about the flakes you panned with Mike?" he asked shrewdly. "I'll take them."

Kathy's heart sank. "How did you know about that?"

Todd shrugged knowingly.

Her gold? No way! But did she have a choice? She needed Todd to help her. There was no one else. She frowned. "Okay," she said. "The gold. But I'll get you for this, Todd Malone. And don't you forget it!"

CHAPTER
14

The next morning, Sharon tapped on Kathy's door to announce that she was leaving for Sunday school.

"Okay," Kathy responded sleepily. "I'll see you when you get back."

Sharon tried the doorknob. "Breakfast is on the table."

Kathy jumped up and unlocked the door. Sharon greeted her with fresh eyes and a rested smile. "After you finish your cereal, help yourself to the cookies. I made extra."

Kathy mumbled, "Thank you." Sharon left. When Kathy heard the car door slam out in front, she ran to the balcony and looked down toward the river. The water looked dark and gloomy, reflecting the heavy clouds that hung over the hills. No sign of Todd—darn!

She hurriedly dressed, bounded down the stairs, and went out on the veranda. No sign of him there either. Turning to go inside, she heard a grating noise on the tower side of the house. She leaped down the porch steps. When she rounded the corner of the house, Todd was standing by the arched door fiddling with the lock.

"What took you so long?" he asked. "And who put this thing on here? It looks new."

"My aunt did, I guess," said Kathy, relieved to see him. "She doesn't want anybody in the tower."

"Yeah, then why are you going up there?"

Kathy shrugged and looked down at the ground. This wasn't the time to tell him about the word TOWER printed in the ashes or about the ghost trying to lead her up the circular stairs. All of that would have to wait. He wouldn't believe her anyway.

"I just have to, that's all," she said firmly. "I might tell you when I get back. Just stay here and watch for my aunt. If she drives up, pound like mad on the door."

Todd let the lock drop, then raised both fists and pounded as hard as he could. "Like this?" he shouted.

Kathy nodded.

"For the gold?" He cocked his head, smiled wickedly, and kept on pounding.

Kathy dug her hands in the pockets of her shorts. "I said you could have it, didn't I? And stop pounding now. It gives me a headache."

He stopped abruptly. "You don't have to look so mad. A deal's a deal."

Kathy started toward the front of the house. "Remember, when you see my aunt's car coming up the hill," she ordered, "start hammering—and not before."

"Sure, sure," Todd said. "How many times do you have to tell me? Do I look stupid or something?"

Kathy couldn't trust herself to answer that one. If she said what she really felt, that she thought he was a jerk to ask for her gold, he would leave. And if he left, well . . .

She looked straight ahead and kept going, past the tower and the high front windows to the porch steps and on up to the veranda. She let the screen door slam behind her, raced up the stairs, then stopped. If she went ahead with this plan and her aunt found out, she would be very, very angry. And if she didn't? A strong feeling in her stomach told her she just had to. No matter what.

Suddenly she felt so alone. More alone than she'd ever felt before. Walking slowly down the hall toward the tower, she wished with all her heart that

Gypsy was with her, cuddled up in her arms, licking her chin.

When she reached the landing, she looked down the circular staircase to the stone floor at the bottom and the arched door. At least Todd was on the other side, and even though she couldn't see him, she knew he was there. Next she peered up the stairs that hugged the tower wall.

"Gypsy," she called hoarsely. "Are you up there?"

She waited and listened. Silence.

When she placed her foot on the first step of the narrow, winding stairs, it creaked. Hesitating a moment, she gulped, then started up.

Creak, creak—up she went, one at a time, counting fifteen steps until she reached the gap where the steps were missing. She stopped and looked over. Whoops! It was a long way to the bottom.

Gripping the rail fastened to the tower wall at her right, she stood and shivered. Could she make it to the next step? The gap must be at least five feet. She tried to extend her right leg far enough and high enough, but it was impossible. No matter how she stretched, she couldn't reach. Not even with her toe.

Letting go of the rail on the wall, she reached for the handrail on her left, the only link between the steps above her and the one where she stood. Sucking in a big breath, she flung her left leg over the handrail, then pulled herself up, straddling the rail in a sitting position. Clenching onto the rail with her knees, she crossed her legs underneath to hold herself steady. As long as she sat perfectly still, she felt safe. But the minute she began shinnying up, the rail shook.

"Whoa," she cried out, clinging to the railing with all her might. But she didn't have a chance. The vibration broke her balance and before she knew it, she had flopped over, still clutching the wooden railing with both hands while her legs dangled in midair.

Now what? She was too far up to stretch her leg back to the step where she had started.

She could try to use the railing like the bars at school and move upward by putting one hand over the other. Glancing down between her elbows, past her feet, and through the gaping center of the tower, she stiffened. It was so far down.

She took another deep breath and slid one of her hands up. The railing shook and she was positive she heard a crack. Her arms ached and her fingers were getting numb. What should she do?

If she could whistle for Todd the way he did for Nugget . . . She placed her tongue behind her bottom teeth the way Mike had shown her, but when she tried to make a sound, only air came through her lips. She tried puckering in her old way, but that whistle was so soft that Todd could not have heard it.

Desperate, she decided to give one big heave. With a grunt she swung out, away from the steps, high above the ground floor. When she swung back, she felt invisible hands give her a boost. That was all she needed for her feet to make contact with the step. She grabbed for the wall railing just as the handrail broke off and fell, crashing to the stone floor, where it lay in splintered pieces.

That could have been me, she thought, turning her face away. She pressed against the wall and waited for her heart to stop thudding. For a second she thought she would throw up. Who had helped her? Who had given her that boost?

A rustling noise above caught her attention. Her courage returned with a surge and she hurried up the two remaining steps to the tower room. When she reached the opening, she brushed aside cobwebs and stepped in.

It was a small circular room. Three windows were set deep into the wall, and below them, window seats were covered with purple velvet. Above the narrow bed standing between two of the windows hung the portrait of Lora.

Kathy stepped back, amazed. The picture looked almost exactly like the sketch she had drawn, except that in this oil painting, a gold locket hung around

Lora's neck and the dress she wore was a much richer shade of green. Her hair was piled high on her head and in her arms she held a bouquet of pink roses.

That's why Lora placed the rose on the plot in the graveyard, Kathy thought.

On a square marble-top table next to the bed, an oil lamp, the one that Lora carried, burned dimly, throwing off an amber glow. She must be close by.

"Gypsy," Kathy called out softly, leaning to the side, peering under the bed.

Nothing. Silence.

She inched her way to the middle of the room and waited. For what, she didn't know. The room appeared empty, but Kathy didn't feel alone. Someone was with her. "Lora," she offered, without moving her head. "I'm here—are you?" Her eyes darted to the right, then to the left.

A scratching sound across the room startled her. If it's a rat, I'll faint, she thought. She turned her head to see what it was. The sound seemed to come from the hearth in front of a small fireplace. Kathy walked over.

Scratch— scratch. The noise sounded like a stick scraping wood. But how could that be? The hearth was made of stone. She kneeled. The sound seemed to come from her right. As the scraping noise traveled, Kathy did too, walking on her knees. When she reached the corner where the hearth met the floor, she spotted a small wooden panel about the width of a shoe box almost hidden from view.

Kathy leaned over and brushed aside more cobwebs, then saw that the wood panel was divided into two sliding doors. Using her fingers, she pushed and pulled, but neither one would slide. She would have to find something to force them open. She gave one more try, and both doors slid open with barely a pull.

The scratching stopped. It must have been meant to lead her to this secret panel. Standing up, she crossed to the table and picked up Lora's lamp. Placing it on the floor, she could see a book inside the compartment. She reached in and brought it out.

It was a very old book with a faded binding the color of dry earth. Lora's name was etched in dull gold at the bottom. Kathy examined it on all sides and took it with her to a window seat. She gazed up at the portrait. "Is this it?" she whispered. "Is this what you wanted me to find?"

Lora's green eyes gazed down on her, and for a moment Kathy thought she saw a hint of a smile cross her lips. Well then, Kathy decided, since she had Lora's approval, she might as well open it.

The first page was black paper. The date, December 25, 1859, was printed in white ink. Below it in handwriting with an old-fashioned flourish it read: *Merry Christmas from yr. devoted sis. Jenny.*

Kathy turned the page. Written on white lined paper in black ink was the date: January 1, 1860.

It was a journal—probably Lora's diary.

On that first day of the year, Lora had described the New Year's Day dinner she and Jenny had cooked and shared. She wrote about how lonely the holidays had been for them without the company of their parents and their only brother, Daniel, who had gone off to San Francisco to build his fortune.

Kathy nodded sadly. It had all happened just like Mike had said. She turned the pages. Lora had written about the town of Riversend and the townsfolk and the church. Then Kathy found the page where the drifter had first come to the Wicklow place. The date was the third of February, 1860.

This should be interesting. She pulled her knees up into a comfortable position, then remembered Todd standing outside the tower door. She hurried over to Lora's cubbyhole in the hearth and slid the wooden panel shut. Then she picked up the lamp and placed it back on the bedside table, careful to leave everything as she had found it—except for the book, which she held securely in her hands. Crossing to the stairs, she started down.

Whoa! How was she going to get down? Now

that the railing was gone, the gap looked even wider. She went over to a window and pushed open a pane. Kneeling on the window seat, she stuck her head out. Todd was sitting next to the arched door tossing a yo-yo straight out in front of him.

"Todd," she shouted. "Up here."

Todd jumped to his feet, shaded his eyes, and looked up. "Hey! When are you coming down? I don't want to sit here forever."

"I can't get down the stairs," she called. "They're missing."

Todd shoved the yo-yo in his pocket. "So how did you get up there?"

"I swung up on the railing," Kathy said. "But that's broken now and I can't use it."

He grinned up at her. "What do you want me to do about it?"

If he asks me what it's worth, I'll strangle him, she thought. But he didn't. He just stood there waiting.

Kathy thought a moment. "It's a wide gap. Can you get the ladder?"

"Not unless I go back to the cabin. Mike borrowed it."

Kathy shook her head. "That takes too long. What if my aunt comes back?"

Todd was thinking now. "How big is the gap?"

"About five feet."

Todd started around the back.

"Where are you going?" Kathy yelled, panicking.

"Hold your horses," he said, sounding like Mike. "I'll find something and bring it up." He took off running, then stopped. "Is the back door open?"

Kathy shrugged, almost getting her shoulders stuck in the open window. "Try it," she said, then added quickly, "just hurry—please."

When he was out of sight, Kathy sat down on the window seat and clutched the journal. If her aunt came back now, she'd send Kathy home for sure. Kathy didn't like disobeying, but how could she make her aunt understand how important all of this was to Lora?

The back door slammed and uneven footsteps climbed the hall staircase. Kathy stood and went to the tower room entrance. Todd appeared on the landing, wrestling a long bench from the redwood picnic table outside. "Can you use this?" he called, balancing it in his arms. Without waiting for her reply, he started up the narrow stairs, grunting all the way.

When he reached the gap, he teetered on the step. Glancing down, he stepped back and leaned against the wall. "Yikes! No wonder your aunt doesn't want you up here. You must be crazy. You could have fallen."

"Todd," Kathy pleaded. "Just help me get down."

She eyed the bench. "Is it long enough—will it reach?"

Holding the bench upright, Todd set one end on the step between his legs. Then he let the top end go. It bounced against the high step above him and rested there, bridging the gap.

"Ta da," he said, holding his hands in the air like a magician. "Nothing to it."

He smiled up at her, then his eyes turned serious. "It should be okay. It should hold, but be careful."

Kathy stepped down and Todd held the bench steady. She stuck the book in her waistband, squatted, then eased her weight onto the narrow bench. Gripping the edges, she scooted herself down a little at a time. When she reached the end, Todd moved over and Kathy stood up beside him.

"Thanks," she said, and meant it. She leaned over and lifted the end of the bench. "Let's get this back."

Todd reached up and grabbed hold of the sides. With a couple of hard yanks they wrenched the top end of the bench loose from the high step. Just as they got it balanced, a slow banging on the arched door echoed throughout the tower like a ghostly warning. Kathy and Todd froze and stared at each other.

Bang—bang—bang—bang.

Todd let go of the bench, pushed past Kathy

taking two stairs at a time, and jumped to the landing.

"Wait," Kathy yelled, letting go too. The bench teetered, slid through the gap, then crashed on the stone floor.

"I'm out of here," Todd hollered over his shoulder. "I'll meet you in back."

CHAPTER
15

Todd was halfway down the hill as Kathy raced to the side of the house and craned her neck to see who was pounding on the door. But no one was there. She started to call after Todd to come back when she heard a car crunching up the gravel driveway.

That must be her aunt!

She pulled Lora's journal from her waistband. Gripping it tightly, she ran as fast as she could down the hill. When she reached the river, Todd was standing on the bank, panting.

"Was that your aunt pounding on the door?" Todd asked, trying to catch his breath. "She sure scared me."

"No," Kathy said, gasping. "Nobody was outside. I just heard her drive up—that's why I ran down here."

Todd looked puzzled. "Then who the heck was it? There's no one else around here." He eyed the book in her hand. "What's that?" He reached for it, but Kathy pulled it away.

"I found it hidden in the tower room," she said, rubbing her fingers along the gilt edges. "This is what Lora's ghost wanted me to find. It's her diary." She carefully opened the book and let Todd get a peek before she shut it again. "Where can we go to read it?"

"Read it?" Todd said in disbelief. "I want to know who was banging on that door. Come on, forget about the book. Let's go back and find out who's up there." He started for the manor.

"Todd—wait," Kathy commanded. "I know who it was. She was warning us so we could get out."

Todd turned and stared at her. "She? Who?"

"Lora," Kathy said.

Todd plopped down on the grass. "You really believe that stuff, don't you?"

Kathy nodded. "It's true. I wish you'd believe me. That banging was so loud. And remember the way it echoed? It was weird. No real person could make a noise like that."

Todd shifted uncomfortably, then nodded in

agreement. "It did sound like something from another galaxy." He searched through the grass until he found a large green clover. "Okay," he said, examining the leaves. "Suppose you're right. Suppose it was her. What does she want with you?"

Kathy patted the book. "I think whatever's written in here will tell me."

Todd jumped up and was greeted by a loud clap of thunder followed by a flash of sheet lightning. "Come on—there's a place up the river." He started out, then stopped. "It's my special place," he warned. "I've never let anybody up there." He looked up at the clouds hanging dark and heavy in the sky. "If you tell where it is . . ."

Two large raindrops splattered on Kathy's forehead. "I won't tell," she promised, shoving the book under her T-shirt. "But let's go. It's starting to rain."

Todd's special place was on the other side of the river, the cliff side. He led Kathy across a narrow part of the water, where boulders were set like big stepping stones. Bounding across, he waited for her on the other side.

Halfway across, Kathy stopped. She wasn't sure she could make it. Falling in didn't scare her since the water was calm, but the thought of ruining Lora's book made her cautious.

"You can make it," Todd said, motioning for her. "They're no farther apart than the others. It just looks that way." He crossed his arms and waited while she made up her mind.

"If I slip, I'll toss you the book," Kathy said. "Just be sure to catch it."

"You'll make it—you can do it," he said. "But if you want, just toss it to me now."

Kathy knew she could throw that far. Her concern was what Todd might do with it once he got it. She didn't quite trust him. She studied the flat rock ahead of her. Its surface slanted and part of it was wet with moss. If her foot hit the upper part, she'd be fine. But if she slipped on the moss . . .

"Here, catch," she hollered, tossing the book to Todd. Then with one jump, she landed where the rock was dry and hopped on the remaining boulders to the other side.

Todd hadn't so much as peeked into the book. Kathy was impressed. "Thanks," she said, smiling. "I'll take it now."

Todd grinned impishly, hesitated, then handed it over. Kathy breathed a sigh of relief.

Todd climbed up the rocky surface until he reached a ledge. Kathy followed. There was an opening in the slate wall. "Is this a cave?" Kathy asked, surprised.

"Kind of." He bent his head and shoulders and went in.

Kathy waited until he poked his head back out

141

and motioned for her. "It goes all the way back," he said. "I keep a lot of my stuff in here. But if you're going to read, we'll have to stay here where we can see."

The two of them sat down near the opening on a pad of dry moss. Before she opened the book, Kathy narrowed her eyes. "I want this to be our secret. I don't want Mike or my aunt to know about what I've found. Promise?"

Todd narrowed his eyes back too. "I don't like secrets—that's what my stepsisters have." He looked angry for a minute. "But I don't have to say anything to Mike," he added. "Your aunt's your problem."

Satisfied that Todd wouldn't tell, Kathy opened the book and showed him the black page with the writing in white ink. Then she pointed out Lora's first entry. She gave him time to read it, then turned pages until she found the date when the drifter had arrived. "This is as far as I got," she said.

"Wait," Todd said, trying to turn back a page. "I want to read about that guy's hat again."

"Later," Kathy said. "I think it's more important to find out what happened on the last day. Here it is." Her voice trembled with excitement as she read out loud.

I sense that beneath his gallant ways lies a violence. Jenny is terribly mistaken if she has any thought

142

that I love him. He wants her to believe that I do in order to divide our affection—and our attention, because it is papa's gold that he is after.

I overheard the two of them making plans in the parlor. They will rendezvous at the river tonight under the big oak. Jenny offered him her inheritance as her personal dowry. He knows my inheritance equals hers and that makes me uneasy.

Another dream came to me last night and I must act on it. Papa, bless his soul, convinced me that I truly have the gift of sight. Not only do I see the present clearly, but in my dreams I can see the past and the future as well. Through the mist of this dream, Jenny was being washed down the river. Dear God, I pray that this does not happen. I am frightened, but I shall follow them to the river with my bag of gold and offer him my inheritance too if he will only be truthful with Jenny. She will suffer a broken heart, but her eyes will be opened to his villainy. Oh, Papa, I wish that you were here to stop this madness, but since you are not, I must do this alone in order to prevent Jenny from ruining her life. Or even worse—from losing it.

God be with me when I confront him.

Kathy looked up with tears in her eyes. Lora had had message dreams. She could see the past and into the future. She'd written in her journal that it was a *gift*. Kathy had that gift too. It was okay!

Todd started to fidget. He grabbed two stones and rubbed them together.

143

"She didn't do it, Todd," Kathy said. "Lora didn't murder Jenny. That's what she needs me for—to clear her name. And that's why she haunts the manor."

Todd listened closely as Kathy went on to tell him in detail everything that had happened while he was away. "I've felt her near me so many times," she said.

"Too bad," Todd said, sounding sincere. "That guy must have pushed Jenny in the river. But if Lora didn't murder Jenny, then what happened to her—and the gold?"

Suddenly they stared at each other. "He killed Lora," they said in unison.

"And then took all of the gold," Todd added.

Kathy crawled outside and stood tall on the ledge. "I've got to show this to Aunt Sharon. She'll believe this." She started to climb down.

"Don't go back yet," Todd called. "Let's see where they found Jenny first. It's not far from here. Maybe we can figure out what happened."

Kathy felt another raindrop. "I'll go if you've got something to wrap around this book. I can't let it get wet."

Todd disappeared into the cave and came out with a plastic bread bag. "Here," he said, handing it to her. "This should do it. I eat lunch up here all the time."

They made their way down the steep grade, then

walked single file along the sandy bank. "We can stay on this side of the river until we get to the river's end," Todd said. "There's a bridge there."

They walked along silently for a while, then Kathy stopped short. "If he killed Lora, then why didn't the men find her in the river too?"

Todd shrugged. "Maybe he didn't drown her. He probably shoved Jenny in the rushing water and Lora saw him do it. Then he took off after her."

"Todd," Kathy shrieked. "You're right! That's why she was running up the hill with the lantern that first night I saw her. She looked so scared." Kathy trembled. "He was after her. I just know it."

Todd nodded hard. "And she didn't make it to the house. Right? You said you saw her turn and run the other way."

"I can't stand it," Kathy said in despair. "Poor, poor Lora."

"There it is," Todd shouted, pointing to an old wooden bridge with rope railings. He took off at a run and Kathy was close behind. When they reached the huge boulders where the river turned, a crack of thunder shook the ground.

"Whoa," Kathy said, staring up at the clouds. "Look how dark it's getting—and I just felt more drops."

Todd ignored her and waded into the river. "I'll bet it was right here. This looks like a muddy spot where a body would catch."

"How gross," Kathy said with a shudder. "I don't like it here. Let's head back." Suddenly the sky lit up. "Don't stand in the water, Todd," she cried out. "You'll get struck by lightning."

Todd immediately jumped out and climbed up on the bridge. There was a cloudburst and the rain poured down on them. Kathy twisted the plastic bag closed as the two of them raced across the bridge then along the other side of the river. As Todd sped past her, he grabbed the bag from her hand. "I'll take this," he said, shoving it up under his shirt. "I'll meet you at the cutoff by the old oak."

CHAPTER
16

The wind arrived in an angry blast, blowing Kathy off balance. She began to run and her foot slipped, almost sending her over the side of the riverbank, but she quickly regained her footing. Overhead, the clouds hung heavy as the storm grew in intensity. The rain was breaking now and hitting her face in waves, making it difficult for her to see more than a few feet ahead.

Where was Todd? When they'd started out, she could hear his feet pounding ahead of her, but now with the wind raging in her ears she could hear nothing. "Todd," she cried. "Wait."

The only sound that reached her was the howl of the wind as it sent debris flying at her head. She stopped and tried to steady herself by stiffening her knees, but that didn't help her upper body. She swayed in the wind like a loose fence post until she could regain enough balance to move on.

She pushed forward while all around her the storm convulsed in shattering light and sound. Thunder bombarded her, but her legs kept moving. When she finally reached the clearing that led up to the manor, she stopped, gasped for breath, and searched all around for Todd. Exhausted, she leaned against the giant oak.

Blue-white lightning streaked the sky and Kathy scurried away. Lightning could strike the tree. She turned and studied the old tree through a gray curtain of rain. That must be the spot where Jenny met the drifter on that terrible night.

A clap of thunder shook her back to the present and she looked around again for Todd. Should she try to go on to the cabin? What if he wasn't there? What would she tell Mike? He might make her stay there until the storm was over and then Aunt Sharon would be worried.

A tiny cry broke through the storm. Kathy cocked her head and listened. It came again like a plea for help. She went back under the tree and looked up. There was Gypsy crouched on a limb, soaked, peering down at her with wide eyes.

"Gypsy," she cried out, lifting her arms. "What

are you doing up there?" Standing on tiptoes, she could just reach the cat's front feet. She tugged on them and Gypsy fell into her arms. "Poor baby," she cooed, cuddling her to her chest. But Gypsy yowled in protest, squirmed loose, then jumped down and raced up the hill.

The water rushed down the slope behind the manor like a shallow river, forking out in every direction. Kathy braced herself and waded ankle-deep against the current, making little progress. Once she stumbled clumsily, then slid backwards, but she didn't give up.

As she struggled toward the crest of the hill, she thought she heard her aunt yell her name. "I'm out here," she called back. But the wind swallowed her words.

Suddenly, lights flickered through the storm and she knew she was close to the manor. To her left, the tower loomed up. Stopping a moment to catch her breath, she saw an orange and white streak cut across her path.

Kathy swerved to the right and chased after Gypsy. The wind was at her back now, pushing her along, making her T-shirt billow out like a wet sail. The cat ran ahead of her and leaped onto the unfinished, ungraveled path. Kathy was right behind her.

"Gypsy," she cried. "Come here—come back."

149

But the cat kept going, darting just out of reach.

Kathy stepped onto the path. When her foot hit the slick dirt, both feet went out from under her. She skidded along the sloped muddy path on her backside, her legs stretched out in front of her. She slid on helplessly with her hair plastered over her eyes until she crashed through a dirt wall, tumbled straight down, and landed with a thud.

Water poured down on her head in bucketfuls. The air was knocked from her lungs, and as she fought to breathe, her mouth filled with muddy slush. It seemed like an eternity before she got her breath back and was able to spit out the mud.

Where was she? As her eyes adjusted to the dark, she was able to make out a dim light coming from above. She looked down at her knees. She was sitting in shallow water on a broken crate in the middle of the floor in the root cellar.

She must have crashed through the weak spot on the top of the mound.

She sat there, exhausted, letting the water pour down her back until she remembered—the rats! When she tried to move, the splintered wood from the crate pinched her hips. What if there were rats down here! What if they were swimming? She had to get over to the wall, where her back would be protected. Bending her elbows and twisting her shoulders, she shoved at the crate.

Free now, she crawled through the water and made it to the wall, where she stood unsteadily. She eyed the brick steps that led up to the slanted door on the mound. Sidestepping along, she hugged the wall and with a sigh of relief stepped up on the bricks where it was dry.

Bending her knees, she stretched her arms and used the palms of her hands to push against the door above her head. But no matter how hard she pushed, the door wouldn't budge.

It must be jammed—or locked!

She rested on the steps, wringing out the hem of her T-shirt, wondering what to do. A huge clap of thunder sounded and she dropped down, put her head on her knees, and covered her ears. When she finally looked up, she saw the hole where she'd crashed through. The water still poured in, but the hole looked smaller.

The soggy dirt on top of the mound must be sliding down and filling the hole in.

As the cellar grew darker, the crates that had seemed so colorful yesterday out in the sun now took on strange shapes in the dim light. One of them even looked like a giant rat.

Kathy shuddered and let out a squeaky cry. It's only my imagination, she tried to tell herself. Tom hadn't seen any rats down here. Why should she?

The only thing to do now was to sit still until

the rain stopped. Then she could empty some of the crates and stack them. That would mean wading out into the water again. She'd have to if she wanted to dig herself out of here. Standing, she tried the door one more time, but all her grunting and pushing wouldn't move it. She sat back down and sighed.

As the hole in the roof got smaller, the water dropped off to a trickle. Her eyes filled with tears and her stomach did a flip-flop at the thought of being down in the cellar without any light at all.

An apple from one of the broken crates floated by. At least she wouldn't starve to death. She reached out and grabbed it, rubbed off the dirty water with the end of her shirt, and took a bite. The light was fading fast. By the time she finished eating, it was almost dark. All that was left now was a peephole.

Maybe she could whistle for help. She placed her tongue behind her teeth, tightened her lips, and practiced. If she could climb high enough on the crates to stick her head out, she could give a shrill whistle. Somebody out there might hear her.

She cleared her throat and tried again. The whistle was breathy and weak. She rubbed her lips. This time her whistle sounded stronger. Trying not to think about the rats, she waded over to the crates and tipped one over. Vegetables tumbled out around her. She emptied one crate after another and stacked them against the dirt wall.

She kept her head to the side, away from the trickling water, as she climbed up three crates. Balancing herself, she carefully stood on top of the fourth. High enough. Using her hand to shield her face, she peered out the hole and saw the rain still coming down, but gently now. She dug at the dirt until the hole was as big as a large grapefruit. Putting her mouth up to the opening, she let out a whistle.

Pretty good, she thought. Not bad at all. But was it loud enough? She tried whistling again, but the dirt started caving in and she pulled back.

If she was ever going to get out of here, she'd have to start digging fast. The crates were shifting and she braced her hands against the wall in an effort to control her wobbly knees. When she regained her balance, she let go of the wall and started digging again. But the faster she dug at the opening, the quicker it closed, until finally the dirt and water broke through with such force that it knocked the crates out from under her.

Crash!

She was back where she had started, shaken and out of breath. The only difference now was that the cellar was pitch black. And the only sound she heard was the drip, drip, drip coming from the covered hole.

Alone in the dark, she was aware of the damp,

dank odor, the same terrible smell that was on the staircase in the house. She reached out like a blind person, feeling around in the water for the crates, but all she felt were vegetables. At least she hoped that's what they were.

Was that a sweet potato that bumped her side? Or the fat body of a . . .

Kathy squeezed her eyes shut.

Please, please, she thought. Just let it be veggies.

As she crawled back to the brick steps, she tried to think of another way out. She couldn't just give up. She had to get out of this dungeon. Her aunt must be worried and looking for her by now.

Or else, Kathy thought gloomily, she found out about her visit to the tower room and now she really didn't care. Kathy shook her head. No. That wouldn't happen. If her aunt didn't find her, what would she tell Kathy's dad? And her mother?

Maybe if she concentrated hard enough, her aunt would know she was down there. She tried to focus, but the musty smell was making it hard for her to breathe, and she felt like gagging. If only there were *some* light.

She pictured her aunt's face and sent out a message to her. *I'm in the root cellar— come and get me.* Visualizing her aunt sitting at the kitchen table, she repeated this over and over in her mind. *Please, Aunt Sharon— help me get out.*

154

A rustling in the far corner of the cellar roused her. She let go of the vision and opened her eyes. A dim light shimmered around a cloaked outline. Kathy gave a sigh of relief. "Lora?" she whispered hoarsely. "Help me."

The ghost floated above the water carrying her lamp. When she reached Kathy, she placed the lamp on the step and gazed at her with loving eyes. Lora lifted her hands and ran her fingers over Kathy just above her skin the way she had done before. Kathy felt the same comforting vibration.

Kathy stood up, holding the lantern. She looked up and Lora's eyes burned feverishly.

"Lora." Kathy's voice was weak. "I read your journal—I know about your dreams. I have them too. You wrote that it was a gift."

Lora looked deeply into Kathy's eyes and nodded over and over again. After a while, she stared down at the water.

"What?" Kathy asked. "What do you want me to do?"

Lora just kept staring down.

Holding the lantern up, Kathy leaned over and stuck her hand in the water. "Is this what you want me to do?"

Lora smiled sadly and Kathy kept swirling her hand around.

She felt something.

Pulling her hand out of the water, she lowered the lantern so she could see. It was a locket on a slender chain, like the one in the picture. "Is this yours?"

But Lora was disappearing fast. She was melting into a white mist that was being swallowed up by the water.

"No, Lora, come back," Kathy cried out. "Stay with me—please."

There was a wrenching noise above her. Kathy looked up just as the cellar door was pulled open and light poured in. She squinted and could make out four figures silhouetted in the opening.

CHAPTER

17

"Give me your hand, Kathy," Sharon cried out.

Kathy reached up and four hands stretched down to rescue her. In just seconds, she was pulled up and out and surrounded by her aunt, Mike, Todd, and Nugget.

"I was sure the banshee got you," Mike said, looking relieved. "That is until Todd here showed us Miss Lora's journal."

Todd hung back and gave Nugget a hard rub on the flank. "Nugget led us to you," he said. "You must have whistled, because there was no way to hold this guy in his stall. He broke through like a rodeo bronco then ran up the hill and stopped here."

As Sharon brushed Kathy's hair back from her

damp face, Mike chuckled and gave his burro an affectionate pat. "Yes sir! That's the fastest I've ever seen him move, especially in the rain."

Kathy smiled at Nugget, then looked anxiously to Todd. "Where's Lora's book?"

"I've got it," Sharon said. "It's safe. There's a lot we have to talk over, but it can wait until later."

Mike squinted at the thin chain dangling from Kathy's clenched fingers. "What have you got there, Missy?"

Kathy opened her hand and the locket fell loose. "It's Lora's," she said excitedly. She held it up by the clasp for everyone to see. "It's the locket in the portrait. Lora led me to it." She pointed down into the dark hole. "It was in the corner of the cellar."

Mike squatted down and peered in. His face grew serious. "When the water goes down, Miss Sharon," he said, rubbing his chin, "it looks like we might have some digging to do. If it's what I think it is, that fella might have done away with her down there."

Kathy let out a small cry and covered her mouth. "As soon as I found the locket," she mumbled, "Lora disappeared into the ground."

Sharon put her arm around Kathy's shoulders and headed for the manor. "It's getting late. You must be starved. There's been far too much excitement around here for one day."

Kathy broke away. "Where's Gypsy? I was trying

to catch her when I crashed through the mound. Is she okay?"

Sharon reached out for Kathy again. "She's fine. When the rain stopped she came to the back door soaked through. I let her in and she darted up to your bed."

Kathy relaxed into her aunt's guiding arm. Mike and Todd followed behind. Before they cut off to go down the hill, Mike stopped. "Miss Sharon, if it's all right with you, I'll be up here bright and early in the morning with my shovel. The water should be soaked in by then. I'll get in touch with the sheriff and we'll find out what's down there."

"Fine," Sharon said, not letting go of Kathy. "We'll meet you over at the mound."

When they got inside, Sharon grabbed a tray from the kitchen, ladled soup into a cup, and followed Kathy upstairs to her room. She made a fire in the fireplace while Kathy took off her wet clothes in the bathroom.

"Just plop them in the tub," Sharon called as she pulled up two chairs. "I'll wash everything tomorrow." Kathy, wearing her nightgown and robe, joined her aunt. She stood shivering with her back to the fire and Gypsy at her side.

"Try some of this soup," Sharon said, pulling the comforter from the bed. "When you're done, I'll wrap this around you." Kathy took two huge gulps from the cup and sat down. When Sharon finished bundling her up, Gypsy jumped onto Kathy's lap, made a slow turn, and settled into the folds of the comforter.

"Kathy," said Sharon as she sat down and put her feet up on the hearth, "I want to apologize for not believing you about the sketch of Lora. I know now I didn't want to believe you. And I know why." She hesitated a moment. "When I was your age I saw Lora's ghost too. I was buddying around with Todd's father at the time and he didn't want to hear about it. Then I went to Mike and he frightened me with his stories about a banshee."

Kathy stroked the white star between Gypsy's ears. "How about my dad? Did he believe you—did he see Lora's ghost?"

Sharon shook her head. "When I was your age, your dad was only four. I told him all about it when we were older. He listened. He didn't disbelieve." Sharon looked down at her clasped hands. "Once I started to tell our mother." She glanced over at Kathy. "Your grandmother. But when she sat down and questioned me, I got scared. I didn't want to be different from the rest of the family. But I think Mom would have understood." She gave a nervous laugh. "She's certainly interested in the unknown now."

Kathy could picture her Grandma Wicklow, the

artist who lived in a cottage in Monterey. She raised an eyebrow. "Grandma believes in ghosts?"

"Your grandmother," Sharon said, nodding, "is quite a remarkable woman. She'll be proud of you when she hears about this." She studied Kathy's face. "I only wish I'd had your courage when I was young. I was afraid to go to the tower with Lora even though I had a deep feeling to follow her. And you know, it's bothered me all of these years. If I had found that journal back then, perhaps I would have . . ." Sharon looked thoughtful. "Well, I might have saved myself a bunch of trouble.

"You know," she continued, "I've traveled all over this country but never settled down. Wherever I went, I always felt drawn back here. When I finally decided to return and nothing strange happened, I was convinced that it had all been my imagination. Then you came and it started up again."

Sharon was quiet for a moment. The only sound in the room was Gypsy's deep purr. "I didn't want to hear your explanations," she said, placing her hand over Kathy's, "because I didn't want to face up to my old fear that this place is haunted."

"Well, it *was*," Kathy said matter-of-factly. "And I liked the ghost. She was kind and beautiful."

"And the ghost liked you, too," Sharon said. "Why wouldn't she? No other Wicklow girl had the courage to help her. If Lora has been trying to clear her name for over a hundred years, she must be happy now. For the first time the family will know that she didn't murder Jenny."

"She loved Jenny," Kathy said. "It must be great to have a sister like that."

The fire had gone down and the red coals gave the room a warm glow. Sharon nodded, yawned, then stood and stretched. "Do you want to bunk with me downstairs?"

"No, that's okay," Kathy said, wanting to be alone. She crossed to the dresser and picked up the GOOD FOR ONE HUG card her aunt had given her the day she arrived. She handed it to Sharon and gave her a squeeze. Sharon hugged her back.

After Sharon left, Kathy climbed into bed and lay quietly with Gypsy beside her, staring out through the glass doors into the night. So much had happened since she'd been here. She got up, went back to the dresser, and took Lora's locket. Reaching for a nail scissors, she carefully pried the locket open. She gazed at the faded, water-stained pictures inside. She could barely make out the images of Jenny and Lora.

Aunt Sharon said that Kathy had courage. But Kathy knew who the really courageous member of the family was—it was Lora, the one who gave up her life trying to save her sister.

She snapped the locket shut and took it back to

162

bed with her. Covering it tightly with her fist, she laid her cheek against her hand on the pillow. "I'm going to miss you, Lora," she murmured as she drifted off to sleep. A familiar vibration brushed against her face and Kathy knew she wasn't alone.

CHAPTER
18

The next morning at dawn, Mike and the sheriff dug in the muddy cellar while Todd and Sharon waited outside.

Earlier, when her aunt had knocked on Kathy's door to ask if she wanted to join them, Kathy had refused. It wasn't that she didn't want to be with Todd and Sharon, it was just that she'd rather hold Gypsy in her arms and watch from the balcony.

Now she was glad that she hadn't gone. When Mike had come out of the cellar with a section of Lora's cloak draped over his arm, Kathy had turned and rushed into her room. She didn't want to see whatever else they found down there.

Lora's graveside service was scheduled for three-thirty. Kathy dressed carefully, wearing the one skirt and blouse her mother had insisted she bring with her. Moving to the mirror, she picked up her brush and stroked her hair. When she was done, she let it fall around her shoulders.

She picked up Lora's locket, all washed and polished, undid the clasp, and fastened it around her neck. The sketch of Lora was propped up on the dresser and Kathy's eyes flicked back and forth from the picture to her own image in the mirror. There was definitely a family resemblance.

If only I could be as beautiful as you when I grow up, she thought wistfully.

A woman's whisper caused her to twirl around. *True beauty comes from within, Katherine. It comes from a courageous heart that's willing to follow its dreams.*

Kathy stood very still and waited as her eyes searched the room for signs of Lora. When nothing happened, she turned back to the mirror. Gazing at her reflection, she mulled over the whispered words. Then she gave a sharp little nod to herself, turned, and went downstairs.

Everyone was waiting in the parlor. Todd looked surprisingly formal in corduroy pants and a bright yellow shirt. Mike had on his best going-to-town red flannel shirt, and Sharon looked absolutely beautiful. She wore a light dress the same shade of green as the one in Lora's portrait, which now hung on the parlor wall next to that of her sister Jenny.

When everyone was ready, they filed out the front door, stepped from the veranda, and made their way down the gravel road toward the cemetery. Todd came up to Kathy and pulled something from his pocket. "Here," he said, holding out his hand. "I figured you might want your gold."

Kathy eyed the glass vial filled with water and flakes. "Thanks," she said, smiling broadly. She stopped and shook the vial gently and held it up. Todd looked over her shoulder at the dancing flakes glistening in the sunlight. Then he took off at a trot and caught up with Mike.

The old gate at the cemetery entrance was open and Kathy was surprised to see that some of the weeds had been chopped down and the leaning headstones had been straightened. She glanced questioningly back at her aunt, but Sharon shrugged and motioned to Todd.

"Mike made me do it," Todd said defensively when everyone looked at him. "You don't think I'd do all that work for nothing, do you?" He scanned the grounds, shoved his hands in his pockets, and moved past Kathy and Sharon.

"That was really nice," Kathy called after him.

The minister from Riversend Community Church was waiting for them at the family plot. He held a

166

Bible open and his expression was solemn. But he couldn't dampen the happiness Kathy felt deep inside. Somehow she knew how Lora must feel right this minute as she waited for them to lower her remains into the plot reserved for her.

The minister recited the service and ended by praying for Lora's soul to find rest. There was no doubt in Kathy's mind that Lora would rest now. When she glanced up at her aunt's face, she knew Sharon felt that way, too.

As Mike dropped the first shovelful of dirt in the grave, Kathy gazed past the open plot to the pine trees on the other side of the metal fence. A dim light shimmering there brightened. Kathy's heart skipped a beat as she made out the vision of Lora. The dark cloak was gone, and Lora stood tall in a dazzling white dress trimmed with gold. She shimmered there, filling Kathy with love. Then the light dissolved into bright particles that floated toward the summer sky.

After the service, wandering along beside her aunt, Kathy noticed as Todd slipped his hand into Mike's. She kept her eyes focused straight ahead until they were up on the road, then she stopped and looked back. The old Wicklow cemetery was quiet now.

The spot by the pine trees where Kathy had last seen Lora was empty, but Kathy's heart was full.

She squinted up at the sky, where the clouds hung like puffs of angel hair. Was that where Lora's light particles had gone? They had been bright and beautiful in the sunlight. In the dark they would sparkle like stars.

If she was the first one to spot a comet some night, she knew what she'd name it. She would call it the *Lora*.

Reaching for her aunt Sharon's hand, she felt the strong family connection between them. She began to whistle happily. Mike turned and did a little jig. Todd watched him and rolled his eyes. Their antics made Kathy laugh, and she lost her pucker. But in that moment she felt connected to them, too.